Year of Grace

A Novel

Margaret Hope Bacon

Quaker Press

OF FRIENDS GENERAL CONFERENCE • PHILADELPHIA, PA

For more information about this title contact:
Quaker Press of FGC
1216 Arch Street 2B
Philadelphia, PA 19107

ISBN: 1-888305-73-8

Printed in the United States of America

Composition and design by David Budmen

Cover photograph "Canoe in the Pine Barens" by Nate Terrell

To order more copies of this publication or other Quaker titles call
QuakerBooks of FGC at (800) 966-4556 or check www.quakerbooks.org

To Chris, John, Annie and Rob

Year of Grace

Chapter 1

FEBRUARY 21, 1968

She had seen this landscape before; the arid terra cotta earth, the bare hills, tawny and low as crouching lions, the fuzz of dry brush. But was it South Africa? Or New Mexico? Or Algeria? It seemed important to know. Perhaps if she remembered she could ask for water in the language of this country. She was terribly thirsty and there were many hills yet to climb.

"Do you want some water?" Unbearable light beat down on her retinas and a face floated toward her, all goggling eyes and large teeth. She was thirsty, but it seemed better to stay a little while longer in the dry, silent hills, dragging her heavy burden behind her, trying to remember the language. "Oui, je voudrais un verre d'eau." But that was wrong here, and would only bring more prying flashlights. Perhaps if she stopped and dug deep into the golden sands she would find water, pure and sweet, bubbling forth.

"I'm just putting a bit of ice between thy lips," a familiar voice repeated near her ear. "It will make thy mouth feel better." And then came the ice itself, wetting her parched lips, cool against her thick tongue. Her sister Jane? But what was Jane doing in Algeria? And where was Tom, just when she needed him? The ice melted and trickled back into her throat, and for a moment she felt sick again, the terrible nausea waiting to spring to the attack, a crouching lion in the grass. But no, it was sinking away, everything was sinking away, and there was only the rustle of insects and the shimmering of light on a vast lake. Uganda? Kenya? Perhaps it didn't matter. Perhaps she could just rest here in the sudden coolness.

"Faith? Faith dear, can thee hear me?" It was morning, curtains fluttered at the window, and her sister Jane was bending over her. Earnest, kindly, good Jane who had never trodden the barren hills. But she did not want it to be Jane, she thought crossly. She did not want to hear any superficial platitudes; she needed someone by her side who had faced the enemy. She tried to slip back into the land from which she had emerged, but the hills and the lake were gone. Instead, unwelcome memories came in bursts; the brilliant, blinding lights overhead, the green turbaned heads bending over her, someone begging her to breathe deeply, and calling her by her first name. "Come on, Faith, you can do it."

"My name is Faith Smedley," she said aloud, "and I have had an operation."

"O yes, dear, thee has," Jane agreed.

"It was one hell of an operation," she said deliberately. There, let Jane make what she would of that.

"O, and are we awake now?" Another set of swishing skirts and bulging eyes. "And how are we feeling?"

The question, Faith thought, was unanswerable unless you were willing to take a poll of all the various selves now coming up for attention; her aching head, her dry throat, the flash of fire across her abdomen, the anchor dragging down her insides. And yet there was still another self floating away from all this, detached, with no intention of landing. Fortunately there was no need to register all this. Without waiting for an answer the skirt was sticking a needle into her bottom, and it was time to sink back to the shores of that shimmering lake.

When she swam to consciousness again it was night, and David was sitting next to the bed, reading the paper. She felt fully herself now, but she was cautious about any movement, and content to lie still and contemplate her son's face in the lamp light. Strong jaw, long face, high forehead. He reminded her of her own father as well as of her husband, Tom. Since Tom was gone, he was the one she wanted near. He had been such a satisfactory son. It startled her to notice that there were crowfeet around his eyes and white in his sideburns. But then, she had to face it, he would soon be fifty.

"Mother, thee's awake." He turned to her now, interested and receptive, but low key. "How goes it?"

"Strange," Faith told him. "I keep feeling as though I were floating off somewhere. How long has thee been here?"

"Oh, I don't know. Which time? Tonight, I've been here since dinner."

"Has it been long?"

"Since Tuesday." He rubbed his cheek. "Thee gave us quite a turn."

Faith stretched her hand to take his solid one, and ran a finger over the golden hairs of his wrist. "I like having thee here. The next time, no Jane. She inhibits me when I'm feeling vindictive."

"I find it rather difficult to think of thee as a vindictive woman," David said. "Shall I get thee something? Thee can have ice."

Faith tried to move her other arm, but found it was strapped to her side. Above, tubes dangled, and there seemed to be a bottle overhead.

"Intravenous?"

David nodded. "Thee will be getting that for a little while, but thee can suck ice, or drink a little gingerale."

Faith felt the pricklings of fear, the fear she had dragged with her up and down the African hills for days and nights now.

"Dr. Stoddard, did he say, does he think . . ." She was suddenly shy, embarrassed as a girl." Did he speak as though he had gotten it all?"

David hesitated in a way she had learned to read. "Of course, mother. But thee can talk to him thyself in the morning."

"Of course," Faith said. So there was something new to think about, to try to face. But she was tired, and the pain was beginning to drag and rend at her again. "Maybe thee ought to call the nurse," she said faintly. "I think it must be time for my next shot."

After that, there was no more retreating to the hills, but a succession of hospital days to be gotten through; the blinding lights, metallic bangs, swishing skirts; the

4

indignities of the bedpan, the predawn tooth brushing followed by the late, cold breakfast, the nurses who called her Faith and treated her like a five year old. She had been through it all before, five years ago, that other time when the doctors said—no, she corrected herself carefully—when she *thought* the doctors said that they had gotten it all and danger of reoccurrence was minimal. She steeled herself now to get through the hospital days by not allowing herself to be annoyed by small things. A wrinkled sheet, a slapdash bed bath, nor to be impatient about the agonizingly slow progress from intravenous feeding to jello and gruel. There was a good deal of pain, but Frank Stoddard had explained that this was to be expected; after all, they had cut out a good part of her stomach. The drugs helped, but they left her with a deep ache and a dry throat. If she drank too much water her old enemy, nausea, swept over her.

And through it all came visitors. Too many visitors, Faith thought fretfully at times. But to whom could she say not to come? Not to her son David, nor her daughters Lucy and Anne, the latter coming all the way from Indianapolis for the operation and returning for a visit. Or certainly not her sister Jane or her brother Harry, who looked crushed and bewildered by her illness. Harry and his wife commuted regularly from Baltimore to see her, and her favorite nephew, Jim White and his tall wife Amelia made a special trip down from Cambridge. And the grandchildren came: David's daughter Peggy, who was studying social work at Columbia; a steady, responsible blonde girl, whose relief was visible when Faith greeted her with a smile and a hug; and Peggy's younger brother Tim, the preppie conservative of the family, home from his sophomore year at Harvard, looking handsome and hiding his concern for her behind bantering words.

Flowers and cards came; from the other grandchildren, from her Friends meeting, from her committees, from old friends. Sylvia brought the first snowdrops, found in a protected corner of the garden in Mt. Ephraim, and Harriet arrived one day with branches of New Jersey high bush blueberries, rosy with rising sap.

"I'm making decisions, and one decision is that thee and I are going to take a long, long canoe trip when this is over," Faith told Harriet. "When the berries are ripe, we'll be there to pick them."

"Does thee think that they'll rent us canoes?" Harriet asked. "Remember the last time when that man thought we were too old?"

"Who would ever think such a thing?" Faith asked. "Thee hasn't changed in twenty-five years." It was true. Harriet had a wizened brown face and straight white hair which she wore with bangs and a bob. She looked perfectly ageless. "Anyway, we can use my cabin at Swallow Creek and there's a shed full of canoes waiting for us."

It seemed important to think about things like canoeing, to make Harriet smile, to make them all smile. But she was tired, and there were so many, many faces.

"You are a popular lady, Faith," the day nurse commented. "I've never seen a patient have so many visitors. Or to be so nice to her nurses. Not one word of complaint. Even when you were out of your head. That's rare."

"My parents brought us up never to complain," Faith said. "They were strict Quakers of the old school."

Although the nurse had grown up in Philadelphia, she had never before met a Quaker, Faith discovered, and had thought they were from up country, like the Amish. Faith found herself giving little lessons on the founding of Philadelphia by William Penn. "Being stoic wasn't just a Quaker thing of course, it was true of that entire generation."

She couldn't readily tell the nurse why she had so many visitors. She didn't understand it herself. Had people always turned to her like this? Well in recent years they had, though she remembered in her youth being quite snippy. And what was it she gave them? At best, a listening ear.

Of course, there was a special reason now. She had seen the reason in David's face that first night of lucidity, and had it confirmed in Lucy's brimming eyes. She waited day after day before questioning Frank Stoddard, wanting to be sure she was strong enough to ask just the right questions.

When the moment came, it didn't seem all that momentous.

"What are these new pills thee has prescribed for me to take after I leave the hospital?" she asked one morning when he came breezing in. He must have come directly to her bedside; it was snowing and a few melting snowflakes still glistened in his hair.

"We're going to build you up very gradually on a little chemotherapy," he said. "It's new, and it's working better than radiation which I know you don't like."

"To try to get the part thee couldn't quite cut out?" Faith hazarded.

Frank looked away. "Just a precaution. It's routine."

"Frank, thee doesn't have to say that." Faith reached out her hand to the doctor and saw to her surprise that he was moved. "I know. The only thing I want to know is, how long do I have?"

The doctor took a deep breath, and looked over her head, at the snowy window. "The answer is, we don't know. I did get the whole tumor, but there was some evidence that it had spread. Perhaps up and down the intestinal tract. It's like a . . . a dispersion of seeds. When it takes, where it takes, how it takes is anyone's guess. The chemicals will keep it inactive for a while. Maybe a year. Maybe more."

"Maybe less?" Faith asked. "It's important, Frank. I've been lying here thinking and I want to do this thing . . . this finishing . . . as well as I know how. There are so many places I want to visit and people I want to see. I want to plan my time very carefully."

"I'd say, count on a year," Frank said. "But I can't tell you how much of that time you'll feel up to much activity. With the chemo you'll feel like you have a mild case of flu."

"I guess I'll just keep going as long as I can."

"That may be longer than you think," Frank said. "You've had a great talent for living, Faith. Even when I was young, in medical school, and blind to most people over thirty, I saw it, the vitality, the shining spirit in you."

"You're thinking, maybe she'll turn out to have a talent for dying as well," Faith hazarded.

"We never know," Frank said gruffly. "Miracles do happen, and new discoveries are being made all the time."

"I really don't mind," Faith said. "I'll be seventy-six in July. It's nearly time, anyway. Only I'm vain enough to want to leave this world with a certain style. Even elegantly."

"Then I'm quite sure that you will."

Chapter 2

JUNE 28, 1968

itting at a desk next to the window in Priscilla Wellington's house in Cambridge, Faith watched the gentle rain dripping from the hydrangeas up against the tiny panes. She could see the heavy burden of moisture gather on each blue petal, watch crystals form at the top, and drop pearl shaped earthward. It was such a miracle to feel as she did this morning, not just alive, not just well, but somehow washed clean, exalted, open to every impression. The blue of the blossoms seemed bluer to her than ever before, she thought, I could just sit here all morning watching those rain drops form. But really, I ought to get on with my letter home.

She had been abroad for over six weeks, and hadn't written a proper letter to her family and friends in that time, just the occasional postcard. There had been so many old friends to see, so many places to visit and scenes to relive that the days hadn't been long enough, and time had flown by. Sister Harriet, who always copied the family letters on her old typewriter, using carbons, would be impatient.

I landed in Paris and Marguerite, bless her heart, met me at Orly and drove me to her very elegant house in St. Cloud, she wrote. *She was ready to wrap me up in shawls and treat me like a very old lady, but I quickly convinced her that that was not necessary. We sat in her garden under a flowering quince tree and I admired her tiny box hedges surrounding her herb garden. My French came flowing back, I am delighted to report, perhaps aided by the glass of wine she gave me. We got reacquainted quickly, and I soon saw she was the same wry, droll, kind woman we had known before. Only perhaps a little heavier, a little puffier when she pulls herself from a chair. Just think, we have been friends for fifty years, ever since the Great War, as they still call it.*

Speaking of the war, Marguerite and her friends are full of indignation about the American occupation of Vietnam, so much more heavy handed they think than their own ever was, they say. And now they are upset about the assassination of Martin Luther King. They followed the student riots at Columbia—so good Peggy was able to go on with her classes—and they are convinced that we Americans have all lost our minds. Well, of course I had to agree with them. You'll remember after Dr. King was shot I didn't feel like coming to Europe at all. But reading about troubles at home always sounds a bit worse overseas, and vice versa. After all, they had their student riots too. We agree it's the price of imperialism, the price France paid for Algeria and and then Vietnam. Why can't we ever, ever learn from experience? But it felt odd and a little sinful to be talking about all this, while sitting in that elegant garden.

She had stayed on in St. Cloud for several days, seeing old friends; a few she had known for almost fifty years, since 1918 when she and Tom had come to Paris to work for the American Friends Service Committee, and had stayed on to close the office. It was strange to see the wrinkled face and double chin of an old man or woman, and then slowly watch the old self emerge as they talked, and the superficial changes disappear.

On Monday, Marguerite's fat son, Anton, and his wife Claire had driven Marguerite and Faith to Pont Aven in Brittany where they and their husbands had once shared a summer vacation, in a small house on the shore, with children running in and out. They stopped at Chartres long enough to see the sun streaming through the rose window, then drove through LeMans, Rennes and Lorient. The apple trees were just coming into bloom, and the tall poplars were leafing out. When they stopped for a proper Parisian picnic at the roadside—folding table, table cloth, wine and all—there were violets in the grass. The Busquets now owned a summer cottage at Pont Aven, and they arrived in the evening. Faith had been more tired by the trip than she liked to admit, but it was heaven to climb into a feather bed and go to sleep listening to the sound of the surf breaking on the rocks below the cottage.

She awoke in the early hours of the morning to the rumble of thunder. The weather was forever changing on the Brittany coast, she remembered. It was almost thirteen years ago that she had been here last, with Tom. They had known then that he didn't have long to live, and they had wanted to revisit some of the places where they had been happy together. O, Tom! Sometimes she still reached out to touch him in the night. If only they had always known how to make each other as happy as they had in those last months. If only she could have always been as fully present for him as she was the day he died.

In the morning, they had visited l'Ecole de Gaugin, and seen the paintings of his followers. It was strange to think of him painting here, so far from his subsequent brilliant scenes in the tropics. And yet the light of Brittany had a luminosity that made colors brilliant, objects stark. "If I stayed here I think I would want to paint," Faith had thought. "I, who could never draw a straight line."

After five days in Brittany they had headed back down the coast of Normandy, stopping at Mont Saint Michael for an omelet at Madame Poulard's. Arriving in Paris Saturday night, they drove along the river, seeing the reflections in the water of the Seine and the brilliantly lit fountains. "City of Light," Faith thought. Was it because she was going to die that everything seemed so much more beautiful this spring?

Marguerite took her to Friends meeting at rue de Vaurigard the next morning. Looking around the small circle of elderly faces, Faith recognized several old friends, wearing those masks of age which disappeared with time. The meeting was almost wholly silent, except for one young American who spoke in very poor French of his despair over the Vietnam War and his disappointment that Friends were not doing more to stop it. Faith thought she would try to speak with him at the end of meeting, but he had slipped away; angry, she supposed, at all the fuddy-duds. Instead, she was kept busy greeting the rest. Some whom she didn't recognize remembered her, and she tried to find appropriate words to say. She grew tired, standing on her feet, and Isabel Mason brought her a chair, for which she was grateful. Later Isabel and Christopher took her home to their apartment for a short visit. After lunch there was time for a nap in their spare bedroom, with a view from the window of tile roofs and chimneys half way across the city. When she awakened, it was tea time, with a number of old friends dropping in for a visit. After the last guests had left they had sat before a cheery fire, while the Masons talked about problems in the American Friends Service Committee for which they worked, and their worries about their daughter, Emily.

"She loved her first two years at Earlham," Isabel said. "And then she began to run out of steam, and spend most of her time on war protests."

"Now she's dropped out completely and is working at a settlement house in New York City for bread, as she puts it, while she continues to do antiwar organizing." Christopher said. "She won't even agree to consider going back to school."

"But what are the children of good Quakers to do at a time like this?" Faith asked them. "She looks at your example and tries to emulate it, that's all."

"But we finished school," Isabel objected. "Well, Christopher had to go back after Civilian Public Service."

"So will Emily," Faith predicted. "Two of my grandchildren are taking a year out."

"Maybe with grandchildren it's different," Christopher said. "With children, it feels so much like it's our responsibility and our fault."

"Yes, being a grandmother is wonderful," Faith agreed, "one feels detached and philosophic. Still parents must know intellectually at least that they have to let their children find their own way."

The conversation turned to Algeria. The Masons had worked in Tunisia among the Algerian refugees at the same time as Faith had worked with them in Morocco, before the war ended and they were able to reenter Algeria. Faith remembered the children and their little faces pinched with hunger. That, and giving out the endless supplies of blankets that came from Quaker meetings, some touching family heirloom quilts donated by loving hands. The Quaker programs were winding down now, and the country was unsettled. They thought it would not be wise for Faith to visit. "At least, let me go with you," Isabel had urged. Faith demurred, then seeing how determined Isabel was to go, she had agreed, although it meant waiting several more days to get a flight to accommodate the two of them.

The several extra days in Paris had been well worth it. The rain had cleared up, and there were two days of perfect spring weather, with the chestnut trees still in bloom. Faith remembered what it had been like fifty years ago, in the spring of 1918. She and Tom were on leave from Grand Pre where they were stationed, Tom part of an *equipe* helping to rebuild shattered homes, while she ran the *ouvroir*, where local women made trousers and vests for sale. It was needed work and useful, and the comaraderie of the unit was fun, but the scenes of devastation all round them were appalling. Sometimes, when the mud melted, the arms and legs of fallen soldiers surfaced. Even her ebullient spirits were sometimes depressed, and it was good to get away.

The sheer excitement of being in Paris, the city she had so long imagined had caused her blood to race, and to be in that city at a time of danger heightened it all. The Germans had Big Bertha trained on Paris, and sometimes bombs fell in the day time. There were often alarms at night, and people still worried about the course the war was taking. The French had seemed picturesque to her young eyes on this first visit, the men with their berets and bicycles, the women dressed in a bewildering array of styles from peasant grandmothers to chic flappers. The streets swarmed with Americans, British, and Canadians in uniform, all young and handsome, it seemed. She too was in uniform, a scratchy Red Cross uniform with a long cape, and the red and black star of Quaker Service on her shoulder. It was hot and heavy, but she knew she looked well in it. Tom, her new husband, told her so, and her own mirror confirmed the verdict, giving her back a girl with red cheeks, auburn hair and sparkling blue eyes.

And then, the gardens. There was never such a city as Paris for gardens, and never such a spring for flowering. Sitting here in the English sitting room, Faith thought that if she could just breathe deeply enough she could smell those chestnut blossoms. And then, suddenly quite unbidden, came an image of Alex, sitting across the tiny table from her at a sidewalk cafe, looking outrageously handsome in his Royal Canadian Air Force uniform, his long legs in polished boots sprawled to one side, and over his head, a chestnut tree, in bloom.

Faith took a deep breath and picked up her pen resolutely.

Algeria seemed far greener than I had remembered it. But of course that was due to the warm, wet spring. The French had mainly left when I was last there; now of course they are long gone, and the Algerians have things back to normal pretty much in the cities. In the country though there is much unemployment and misery. They have never really resolved the question of what to do with their vineyards. What irony; a travesty of colonialism, the French turning a Moslem country into one big winery.

In Tlemcen, they had found a small foreign hotel still operating, and Isabel had arranged for them to rent a Deux Chevaux. The next day they toured the city, Isabel driving while Faith pointed out familiar landmarks. In the old quarter, they found the team's cook, M'Barka, who laughed and cried at the sight of Faith. She insisted that they stay to dinner. Faith wasn't sure she could manage it; squatting on the floor and dipping lamb stew from a common bowl with her fingers, but when M'Barka said she was inviting her married daughter and new baby grandchild to come, Faith knew they couldn't refuse. On the way home to their hotel they saw a wedding party dancing through the streets, the men snapping their fingers and playing bagpipes or waving sparklers. They stopped to watch, entranced, and Faith remembered her first impression on coming here of entering a completely different culture, and rejoicing that the human experience could be so varied.

They had arranged to turn their car in at the airport at Oran, and had a little time to kill. They had bought bread and cheese and grapes for lunch, and thought they would like to eat it beside the sea, where it might be cooler. They turned down a road which Faith thought she remembered and passing through several abandoned grape arbors came abruptly to an old army installation, a fort which once covered approaches from the Mediterrean. No one seemed to be anywhere around. They climbed out of the car and mounted the steps to the cement platform. The war was only six years ago, but already the cement was crumbling, and little feelers of wild vines were reaching between the cracks. A few rusty canons lay in thick grass, close to their former mountings. Aside from the moaning of the wind, it was completely silent.

"So much for man's invincibility," Isabel said. Faith looked at the widening cracks at her feet and wondered how soon a tree would take root in the growing fissures.

At the airport there was a moment of suspense while the Algerian soldiers discovered that Faith's visa had expired a few days earlier, but in the end they were roughly waved on. The plane put down in Geneva, where Faith disembarked, parting with Isabel, who was going back to Paris. Faith was beginning to be more than a little tired, and suspected that M'Barka's lamb had been too hard on her poor stomach, but she had promised to visit the Knights, a British couple she and Tom had met in the early days in Paris.

"You look like you could use a rest," Lydia Knight said after they had greeted her at the airport and retrieved her luggage. "We're going to let you rest for a day or so, and then we thought we'd go up into the mountains to our little place, and have some days of doing absolutely nothing."

"That sounds wonderful," Faith agreed. She *was* tired, she admitted, and she was glad to reach the peace and coolness of the Knight's beautiful apartment overlooking the lake. The Knights had stayed on after World War II and Hugh now had an important position in the United Nations office in Geneva, which involved their giving, as well as going to, many diplomatic parties. Lydia however had arranged for no one to come in that afternoon, and after an early supper, Faith was glad to retire to the guest bedroom and sink into a long, dreamless sleep.

She was rested enough the next day to enjoy the car trip up to the French Alps, and enjoy the growing freshness of the air. In May, there was still melting snow to be seen along the way, and avalanche lilies growing in the trickles of melting ice water. After Faith had rested for a day or so, they began to take cautious climbs in the hills near the Knight's chalet, carrying their picnic lunches in knapsacks on their backs. One day, they found they were sharing their flower strewn mountain meadow with a bull. He looked over at them, tossed his head, and snorted, but he was among his cows and too placid for warfare.

"I'm feeling so well now I can't believe I've been sick," she confided.

"It's the mountain air," Lydia Knight ventured.

"That, and the good company," Faith agreed.

It would have been nice to believe that she was miraculously cured, but Faith knew better. When the adventure was over and she reached London she dutifully checked in with the Harley Street doctor Frank Stoddard had recommended. He examined her carefully, spoke of partial remission, but gave her another set of mild chemotherapy pills to take for a week. She decided to hole up in a London hotel for the ordeal, spending long, lazy days in bed, reading the paper, reviewing all the plays she might see if she felt up to it, and ringing room service for an occasional pot of tea and toast.

So here I am finally after this much too long narrative, Faith wrote. *I have found the funny little house we rented in 1930 when Tom was here on sabbatical, visited the day school were Lucy and Anne were enrolled, drove to see David's proper public school, been to say hello to the swans, and of course gone to Quaker meeting. It is hard to remember that was almost forty years ago, and that you, whom I see vividly here as rosy cheeked children in high stockings, knickers or pleated skirts, are now very proper adults.*

Faith laid her pen down. Her hand was cramped from writing. And it was hard to know what to say next. Suddenly, the easy flow of words was blocked. There was such a welter and conflict of memories here—happy memories, sad memories, secret memories. There are so many things I will never share with anyone, she thought, even though I am going to die soon.

March. Had it been March? Faith remembered a rainy cold day with the wind plastering her wet skirts about her legs and water sloshing in her overshoes. She had gone to take Lucy's forgotten Wellingtons to her school, and was coming back along the river, using her umbrella as a shield against the wind and the driving rain. She could barely see her way, and she ran straight into a tall figure on the bridge.

"O excuse me, Miss," the man said. And then, exultantly, "But it's Faith!" And there was Alex, beaming down at her, water streaming from his dark red hair, his face seeming very close, and bringing back suddenly all the excitement and danger of Paris, and the rue de Rivoli, and chestnut trees in bloom.

They stood there, grinning, searching each other's faces, while the rain beat down on them. It seemed so good, so natural to be with Alex again, that Faith's heart stopped racing, and as soon as she got her breath, she invited him home for a cup of hot tea. Once inside the cottage she was suddenly attacked with panic. It had been a near thing in Paris; it had taken her months to get over him. She must not get involved again. But, surely, she reminded herself, she was no longer a flighty girl not settled into marriage yet, but a contented matron of thirty-eight with three children in whose lives she was engrossed. Surely all danger was past. Tom came in shortly, and they had tea laced with a little brandy to ward off getting a chill. Tom hadn't seen much of Alex that first time in Paris, but now the two men got along famously. Faith looked from one to the other, her heart full. Alex told them about his wife Priscilla and their two children, and the very next day they were invited to the Wellingtons for dinner.

Priscilla had seemed stiff at first, a very proper English matron, but Faith soon got used to her and saw that it was partly shyness that gave her that manner. The two couples got along well, and began to spend all their time together, taking the children with them on picnics and trips to the London zoo. Faith was unreasonably happy, and yet it all seemed innocent and joyous.

Only, she had been wrong about the danger. She found after a few weeks that she and Alex were looking at one another, their eyes speaking a secret language of their own. One day, when Priscilla was in London, shopping and Tom was teaching a class, Alex had taken her punting on the river, with the willows trailing their branches into the water and swans swimming by. They tied up for a bit by the side of the river, and Alex took her hand, and looked at her gravely. "O Faith," he said. Faith found herself babbling, confessing how often she had thought of him since that spring in Paris.

After that, they began to arrange times to be together. To talk, they said, but their feelings were too strong for talk. They were both determined not to hurt spouse or children, to end this thing now, immediately, but each meeting seemed to enmesh them further.

Almost forty years ago, and yet the memory of those three months in Cambridge was still vivid. For years she had remembered it all as though it had happened yesterday, each scene when they met, each thing Alex had said. Despite her efforts to discipline her thoughts it had taken only a slight jolt to turn the tape on. After she and Tom had found each other again, it had begun to fade, but now, coming back here it was all sharp and clear again. Perhaps revisiting the scene of so much turmoil had been a mistake.

A scratching at the door, plus a sudden frantic fit of barking by the Wellingtons' terrier announced the return of Priscilla.

"Love, Mother," Faith scribbled hastily at the end of her long letter. Better get it into the mail before she remembered any more things she didn't want to write about.

"You've almost let the fire go out," Priscilla scolded, coming into the room, pulling off her wet gloves. A tall, handsome woman, she still had that air of absolute assurance that had initially frightened Grace years ago. The fear of course had been mixed with guilt, never being quite sure how much Priscilla had known or suspected about herself and Alex. Priscilla would not only have been hurt, she would have disapproved. Yet Faith liked Priscilla, and the fact that they had both loved the same man had been a bond. After Alex died, so many years ago, she had written to Priscilla, and they had thereafter kept in touch, until a genuine friendship flowered. At first she had thought that sooner or later they must talk about herself and Alex, but whenever Faith approached the subject, Priscilla veered away. If it were a secret between them, it was to be a hidden secret. After a while, it no longer seemed to matter that much.

"I don't quite know why we insist on keeping everyone alive forever," Priscilla said now, stooping to add another scuttle of coal to the fire. "If we go on like this we'll have an entire population of young people laboring to support a generation of old fools."

"How was your sister?" Faith asked mildly.

"Ornery and unreasonable," Priscilla replied. "She doesn't like the matron, she wants the curtains in her room washed immediately, she criticizes every meal. Minutely. And, oh Faith, I remember her when she was really a fine person. I just think it would have been better if she had died right after she had that stroke."

"Life is a very precious thing. I guess it is pretty hard to let go," Faith said. She was aware that Priscilla had not been *notified*.

"I suppose I'll be worse," Priscilla said. "And not very long off, either. I'll be seventy-five next month."

"You're younger than I," Faith exclaimed. "That's news. And here I've always been a little in awe of you."

"Of me?" Priscilla laughed. "There's nothing to be in awe of, I assure you. In a way, this thing with my sister is the hardest I've ever faced, and I'm failing, miserably."

"Henrietta really bothers you that much?'

"Sometimes I hate her," Priscilla spoke vehemently. "And then I hate myself for hating her. I feel trapped by her dependence and I ask myself, where else do I want to go? What else do I want to do? After all, Alex is gone and now the children are gone. She's the only person in the world who truly needs me. But when I am with her I have this great urge to reform her, my own older sister, shake her out of the narrowness into which she has settled." She laughed bitterly. "I read her things about Vietnam and starvation in Africa, just to see if I can't get her to think about someone's troubles besides her own. Of course, it doesn't work, and it makes me madder."

Faith sighed. "She never had much beside her teaching and her books, did she?"

"No, I suppose this was coming from way back," Priscilla said. "Nothing ever happened to stretch her."

"Like having an older sister to care for?" Faith asked.

Priscilla looked at her. "You know, Faith, you've grown into a wise woman," she said. "Were you always wise?"

"Not always," Faith said. "In fact, quite unwise, many times." Did Priscilla know, or even suspect what she was thinking of? "But sometimes things happen which force you to think. Now was there some talk of tea?"

"What an English woman you've turned out to be," Priscilla got up and stretched her arms above her head. "You've managed to make me feel better about myself, as usual. There'll not just be tea, there'll be tea with scones."

Chapter 3

OCTOBER 15, 1968

"Has there ever been such a glorious day?" Faith asked. She held her dripping paddle above the water and turned to face Harriet, steering so earnestly in the stern of the canoe. "Does thee think we've died and gone on heaven, as Tom used to say?"

Harriet paused just a moment, then smiled with delight. Faith had been working at it in the past month, using the word death whenever it came up, casually, so that there might not be that shadow between them. Now instead they could remember Tom as the gangling country boy from Maryland they had met their junior year at Westtown. "Have died and gone to heaven," he would say, over a cup of chocolate after skating on the lake.

"The colors are so brilliant I feel like shouting," Faith said, resuming her paddling. "Does thee suppose they've ever been this bright before?"

"It seems that way, every year," Harriet said. "This must be the peak, though, this weekend."

They were paddling along Swallow Creek, in South Jersey, near Faith's summer cottage. The swamp maples, with their feet in the water, had begun to turn scarlet as early as September and now, in mid October, a whole orchestra of colors had joined in; the red of sour gum, the vermillion of sweet gum, the gold of oak, the burnt orange of bracken, the rose of blueberry, and above all the deep serene blue of a cloudless sky.

Somewhere, far away, a crow cawed, and then a truck changed gears on the road past the store. And yet it was still so still that Faith found herself dipping her paddle with care so as not to make the slightest noise. It's like . . . it's like love, she thought, that tremendous moment of silence before ecstasy. Heavens, what a thing for a seventy-six year old woman to be thinking!

"I wonder why the water always gets so light at this time of year?" Harriet asked. "Notice how one can even see the bottom now?"

"I think that lovely cedar color comes from little decaying particles of matter, and when the first frost comes they die," Faith said. "At least, I think that's what David told me. I like to watch all the little leaves whirling along in the current, like confetti."

The little river, cut deeply through a terrain of sand, meandered like a corkscrew. It was swift and deep, and many unwary novices had tipped over in trying to maneuver the curves. For Faith and Harriet however, after almost fifty years of experiencing canoeing together, it was easy. They paddled smoothly in unison to round a bend. Before them two chickadees flew from shore to shore, chirping.

"Doesn't thee think we might turn back now?" Harriet asked hesitantly after a bit. "The current will be against us and the sun will be down before we reach camp."

"I just want to see the place where the man fell in," Faith said. "We always made that the turning around place when the children were little."

"I never knew, who was the man?" Harriet asked.

"I never knew either," Faith said. "Some friend of Tom's uncle. He looked so pompous there on the dock, casting a line into this river where no one has ever seen a fish. I think he had on a striped suit and one of those old panama hats. And then suddenly, whoosh! There he was in the water, gasping like a Florida blow fish."

"It's such a surprise when it happens to you," Harriet said. "I remember once I had someone come down from Irving's office who had never canoed before and I drew him as a partner. I've never seen such an awkward man. 'I'm getting it, I'm getting it,' he kept saying, splashing me with every dip of his paddle. And then suddenly we both got it, a dunking. The river was cold, too."

They were quiet for a bit, paddling smoothly. They had come to a place where tall cedars lined the stream, and interlaced their branches overhead. The restless current, slicing into banks of sand, had undercut the roots, so that the trees leaned across the water. Someday they would fall. Now the stretch of river had the feeling of a vaulted cathedral. The two women glided through in hushed silence.

Next they came to a bend in the river, where the water widened out into a small pool. A dock jutted from the farther shore.

"That's the place where the man fell in," Faith confirmed.

"Is thee tired of sitting? Want to get out for a bit before we go back?" Harriet asked.

"That's not such a bad idea," Faith acknowledged.

They approached the dock, tied the canoe to a post, and climbed out cautiously, one by one. They were both stiff and uncertain on their feet after sitting so long in one position. In a few minutes they decided to climb to the cabin, mounting cautiously on the steps of cedar logs.

Like almost every other cabin on the creek, this one was owned by old friends of theirs. Philadelphia and New Jersey Quakers had settled this creek for weekend vacationing shortly after World War I. The families knew each other well, many having gone to school together, and many being related. With better roads to both the Pocono mountains and the New Jersey shore, most of the families had all but deserted their cabins now. Some came down only in the spring for birding, and in the fall for the leaves. One or two had sold their property to strangers outside the magic circle. Such sales had to be approved. There was a residents' association which owned hundreds of acres of wilderness surrounding the creek, and which oversaw the sale of properties.

"The poor Carters practically never get down here anymore," Harriet commented, seeing if she could peer into the cabin through the shutters. "And the children now all go to that place in Vermont. They keep trying to get Margie to sell it, but she won't hear of it."

"Remember the time we came down here after graduation and played that game of blowing a ping-pong ball at each other across the table?" Faith asked. "It turned out that one of the Brinton boys was incubating chickenpox and we all got it exactly two weeks later."

"No, I had forgotten that," Harriet said. "What a time that was. Faith, thee has a remarkable memory."

The cabin, like all the others, was sheathed with cedar shingles, and had a wide front porch. The two friends sat together on the top step. From here, the full sweep of the bend in the river was in view. The water, catching the setting sun, was sheer amber. A maple, all crimson and coral, blazed like a flame on the far bank, and its reflection was so pure that it appeared to be falling, like a volcano of fire, into the creek.

"I can't believe that we are really here," Faith said, "and that they are actually going to let us stay."

She had come home from Europe in July, into a nation still in shock and mourning from the death of Robert Kennedy. It was hot, and Philadelphia was dirty and full of anger. She felt sick and defeated, and the third course of pills made her ill. She had spent a few days in her bed in the house at Haverford, the blinds drawn, ready to give up. But by the end of the week she was enough better to face visiting David and Margaret at the Cape.

Over dinner one night, she mentioned, as casually as she knew how, her plan for spending the fall and winter at Swallow Creek. David seemed to accept the idea at first, but Margaret argued against it, and he came around to supporting his wife. It would be impossible to winterize the drafty old cabin sufficiently. The sand roads were in poor shape and there was every chance they could be snowed in. Harriet Buffum was a nice old thing but scatterbrained; she would be no help in an emergency. What if the power went off, as it often did, for a long period of time? No, it was a lovely idea, but not very practical.

"None of us would have a moment free from worrying about you," Margaret said.

"I don't want to be the cause of worry, but I do want to spend this year the way I choose," Faith said carefully. After all, they must see that if she were going to die she had the right to plan her own last months.

Lucy and Bert arrived from Boston the next day, were evidently told of mother's crazy plan, and also balked. There was the house in Haverford, what was she going to do with that?

"Close it up and put it on the market," Faith told them. And what about her boards and committees? What about meeting? "I am certainly not going to spend this year going to committee meetings," Faith protested.

But the grandchildren argued for grandmere's right to make her own decisions, and her youngest daughter Anne, consulted by long distance phone, was immediately favorable. Mother had always been reasonable, she pointed out, and if she wants a little fling of her own planning, well, what business is it of ours? Her voice broke, and David put the phone down thoughtfully.

Other people objected, including Faith's lawyer and her doctor, Frank Stoddard. Even Harriet Buffum's children were worried. Mightn't it be too much for Harriet? She had always feared sickness and death. Faith wondered if she was being selfish and causing too much trouble, but the passage of time made her feel that for her this was a right leading.

"It's my own death," she told herself, still getting used to the word, "let me do it in my own way."

Back in Haverford in August, she almost weakened. She had been trying for years to simplify and throw away, but there was still so much to deal with. Was this what life really amounted to, the accumulation of mounds and mounds of objects? She could of course simply sail out and let the children clean up and sort out and throw away after she was gone, but this seemed to her hardly fair. Instead she went through drawers and cupboards, ruthlessly throwing out whatever was of questionable value, developing piles of things to be given to friends, more things for the Haverford library. In each room she marked the furniture that had already been spoken for—the old mahogany table for David and Margaret, the grandfather clock for Lucy and Bert, the dear old rocking chair for Anne.

Next to Tom's old bureau she piled things she couldn't bear to part with. There was the sand dollar they had picked up at Atlantic City on the first day of their honeymoon. David's first baby gown. (Give it to David and Margaret for their grandchildren?) A diary she had kept sporadically that year they spent in France for the Service Committee. (Give it to the archives? But she had better read it to be sure that there wasn't mention of Alex.) The graduation program at Harvard when Tom got his Ph.D. The menu from a restaurant they had gone to in Annecy to celebrate their twenty-fifth wedding anniversary. A letter

Tom had written to her when it seemed possible that their marriage was about to unravel. Burn it? Read it once more before burning it? David and Margaret's wedding announcement. There was a whole box of papers about the White family her father had left her, and which she had promised to read before turning them over to Haverford. And on and on. After a while she decided to get several file boxes, and take the things with her to Swallow Creek, where she could decide in peace.

Margaret, who was efficient, if a trifle bossy, came and worked with her. Even Peggy spent a couple of days sorting books. In shorts and a tee shirt, with her long hair clubbed into a single braid, she looked very much like the small blonde solemn girl Faith had known as her first grandchild, a female replica of David. Peggy was very much a White, and she examined the old family portraits with reverence. Faith made a mental note to review her will and see if she could leave them to Peggy.

At the end, Faith's old maid, Rosie, came back to clean, and brought a young niece. They had a spell of true Philadelphia summer weather, hazy, hot and humid, and Faith felt weak and sick frequently. They kept the radio turned on, and Faith found herself charged with anger as she listened to reports of police violence at the Democratic National Convention in Chicago. She would like to lecture those policemen, give them a lesson in American history, tell them what her Quaker ancestors had endured to protect the right of free speech. Lucy, who called almost every night, said they were quite sure their son Charlie was out there, and Faith watched the television coverage nightly, afraid that she would see his face. The world seemed very much out of kilter. Did she have the right to simply slip away and escape it? But she kept on doggedly, and the piles ready for dispersal grew as the old rooms slowly emptied.

David had meanwhile taken over the job of winterizing the cabin at Swallow Creek. He and his architect friend, John Bishop, had spent a long day there, measuring and jotting, and as a result John had drawn up a plan which Faith liked. The big living room and two bedrooms were to be insulated and paneled with rough pine planks, a bathroom added, the kitchen remodeled, a garage added with an attached bedroom. Even the cathedral ceiling had to be insulated, but John found an imaginative way to do this so that the heavy beams still showed. Otherwise he kept things much as they had been, except for enlarging the window that looked out over the river.

"I think putting in the phone was one of the things that convinced them," Harriet said. "That and adding the extra bedroom in the garage in case we ever need live in help."

"And I was able to convince them that we had neighbors nearby in case of emergency," Faith said. "The Paxton's store right up on the main road."

"And Angelina and Juan at the blueberry packing plant," Harriet added.

Shortly after they had arrived they had found a local woman to come in twice a week to clean and do the laundry. Angelina was a Puerto Rican who had come to Swallow Creek originally with her husband Juan to work in the blueberry fields. After several seasons the manager of the packing plant had asked Juan to stay on in the winter as plant watchman, and they had settled in a cabin adjacent to those occupied by the migrants in season. Faith had gone to pick her up a couple of times and was shocked by the squalor of the camp. The Costas had a separate cabin near the rows of shacks that housed the migrants, but it looked to be in terrible condition, the entrance step at a crazy angle, one window boarded up. There was a water tap that served the whole camp and two rickety outhouses. But Angelina was well scrubbed and dressed in freshly laundered clothes, and the wash she did for Faith and Harriet came back crisp and sweet smelling. Faith knew she ought to be concerned about conditions in the camp, but it had been there, just the same, all her adult life, and now was perhaps a bit late to start in on a fresh crusade.

"If thee is rested, we really ought to turn back now," Harriet said.

"Harriet, thee is not to fuss over me!" Faith said, reaching out for her friend's hand. "Really, dear, we will be miserable if thee is going to feel responsible. It isn't a natural role for thee and it bothers me a good bit. After all, I chose thee for this winter because we've always been so easy together. Let's not risk it now, shall we?"

Harriet's leathery face relaxed. "It's the children, both thine and mine. They keep telling me what I must or must not do."

"Oh, the children," Faith waved her hand. "First they tried to manage their own children and then when they failed they try to manage us. Such an uptight generation. I feel much more relaxed with my hippy grandchildren."

"Are they all hippies?" Harriet asked innocently.

"They come in all flavors," Faith told her. "Anne's got a son who has joined an Eastern religious sect. And Lucy and Bert have a revolutionary. He tells them their middle-class way of life is part of the problem. Quakers and pacifists are petty bourgeois deviationists, or whatever the New Left calls them. He was in Chicago at the Democratic National Convention and got arrested. Then there's David's Tim, who is straight as an arrow, and will vote for Richard Nixon. The rest range in between."

"Sounds like they at least talk to you," Harriet said. "My grandchildren are always so polite I never know what they're thinking. And yet my heart goes out to them so."

The sun was indeed beginning to set, and the colors to deepen. Faith and Harriet climbed down the stairs, helped each other carefully into the canoe, and paddled silently upstream through a blaze of amber and coral. Above them the colors bled to the west, leaving the sky pale. Just as they rounded the last bend, a star pricked its way out above the cabin roof.

Chapter 4

OCTOBER 28, 1968

As far as I can ascertain, our ancestor, Joseph Burgess White, arrived in the Massachusetts Bay Colony in 1636, and settled in the vicinity of Salem, where he took up farming. A brother, Nicholas, emigrated at a somewhat later date, and moved to Barnstable. Aside from the births of his children, there is little recorded about Joseph until 1659, when he accompanied Isaac Robinson to Plymouth, charged by the General Court to "seduce the Quakers from the errors of their ways." Instead, Isaac and Joseph were both themselves seduced, according to the old records. They became Quakers and thereby exposed themselves to the intolerance of the times.

Faith looked up from the manuscript, written in her father's precise script, and smiled. "Exposed themselves to the intolerance of the times." How like her father that phrase. With his rimless glasses, his tightly furled umbrella, his rubbers, he was no man to expose himself needlessly to any risk. She remembered one morning before his eight-thirty class, Annie on her knees mopping at her father's trousers where a cup of tea had accidentally been spilled, her mother chiding gently, "Now

Joseph dear, be calm," the unrepentant puppy gamboling about, her sister Jane in tears, Harry with his head down, staring into his lap. A Quaker household surviving a crisis. It was hard to put together this image of her father with the stirring tales about early Quakers enduring persecution. And yet, wasn't it her own father who had gone, tightly furled umbrella and all, to see the President when they had learned that some of the conscientious objectors who were drafted into the army in World War I were beaten for their beliefs?

As we know, her father's manuscript continued, *Several Quakers from Salem were subject to imprisonment or disfigurement at this time when they persisted in going to Boston to preach the Quaker message. In fact, four of them were hanged. Our ancestor was evidently not led to participate in these ventures. On the other hand, there is a record of a Joseph White being imprisoned in Salem in 1661. Shortly thereafter, with his wife and two children, he fled the colony.*

"Harriet?"

"M'nn?" Harriet, sitting on the other side of the picture window with her knitting in her lap, looked up patiently. Faith had spent the morning rummaging through the White family papers she had brought along, and reading Harriet excerpts. Some, Harriet's expression said, were more interesting than others.

"Harriet, can thee imagine being a young wife with two small children, and probably pregnant with a third, having to pack up all thee owned and go off into a wilderness full of wild beasts and savages, accompanied by a man who refused to carry a gun?"

"No, I can't imagine."

"I've never really thought about it before," Faith mused. "Forests with no roads, just deer tracks or Indian paths, and lots of bear and panther, and Indians who had never seen a white man, Quaker or otherwise. And no way to keep warm, except perhaps for a little fire at night, and no hot water to wash the baby."

"They must have had a lot of faith," Harriet said. "They lived on faith."

"We really can't imagine it," Faith said. "We just can't visualize it, can we? When you read the old journals they talk about being led by the Lord in a way we don't really begin to understand any more. Imagine being willing not only to risk one's own life, but the lives of one's children. I just can't put myself into their frame of mind."

"It is hard to imagine," Harriet agreed. "But haven't some people always been willing to risk everything for an idea? For politics or art or music?"

"And there wasn't much else going on in the seventeenth century besides religion," Faith said, "at least for the common people. Anyway, according to my father's account they had a terrible time. They stopped for awhile in East Jersey and he tried to farm but there was a drought and they didn't prosper. More babies were born, and several died."

"They didn't keep journals?"

"If they did, they've been lost. No letters, either. Nothing here from either of them, except meeting records, and Joseph White's deed when he bought the land in Cumberland County from the Indians, and his last will and testament. He left everything to his wife, which I suppose is a sign of a good marriage, and Quaker respect for women. In those days most men left their land to their sons, but I gather he had already provided for them. It is so hard to read between the lines and have any idea of what they were really like."

"Does it matter?"

Faith took off her horn rimmed glasses and laid them on the table before her. It was hard to explain to Harriet, even to herself, but yes, it did matter. She had promised her father to go through these family papers, and this, she decided with ironic humor, was the last chance she would get to fulfill that promise. But there seemed to be more at stake than being a dutiful daughter. More and more she found herself trying to know these ancestors as human beings, and to look for the threads that had held their lives together.

She was aware that she had lapsed into thought and that Harriet was watching her, waiting for an answer. "I've never thought much about my family background before," she told her friend. "Father was so obsessed with genealogy, it seemed to us, and so pedantic about it that we all just stopped listening when he started in. But I felt sorry we had been so unfeeling about it after he died. It was his great anxiety at the end that he hadn't completed the task and given the diaries and the letters to the Quaker Collection at Haverford. So I told him I'd take it on. And now, I find I'm really interested. After all, they are my heritage. They probably influenced my life in more ways than I know, and they go on, influencing my children and my grandchildren."

"What thee ought to do, is write thy own memoirs," Harriet said decidedly. "Thee's had a fascinating life, and thee's influenced more people than anyone I know."

"No," Faith shook her head decisively. "I haven't come to enough conclusions about life. I'm not old enough yet." She laughed. "But I've saved a few of my letters from abroad, and I'll give them to Haverford along with the rest. And maybe some day some great grandchild will go rooting about, trying to find out about me."

"Now then, how about a cup of coffee," Harriet said briskly.

"Is there some left from breakfast?"

"No, but it won't take me a minute to make a cup."

"Never mind, I think I'll just move around a little."

Faith got up, feeling stiff. She had been sitting by the window, her feet up, reading for several hours, resting her eyes occasionally by looking out toward the river. It was a cool, gray day in late October. The sky had a luminous, pearly quality, and the fall colors, subdued now to somber browns, russets and golds, glowed as though lit with an inner light. The familiar view of the river from the window—the wide sweep around the bend, the glint of ripples as it narrowed, the lean of a giant cedar on the bank above—always refreshed her.

As she stood there, she felt a sudden jagged thrust of pain in her back. My back? She flinched, and waited quietly for the spasm to go away. Everyone my age has hundreds of aches and pains, she reminded herself. I mustn't panic.

"I think I'll make myself a cup of instant coffee after all," she announced, walking across the room with care, to turn up the flame under the kettle. "No, my secrets will die with me. But that's what makes me curious. When these Whites wrote, they were so formal and proper. I wonder how many of them really had secrets in their hearts."

"Does thee really have secrets?" Harriet asked.

Faith smiled. If ever there had been rumors about her, dating perhaps from her first fling with Alex in Paris in 1919, Harriet would have been the first to dismiss them, the very last to know.

"Oh, maybe one of two," she said noncommittally. "But back to the Whites, I wonder a lot about Martha. Was she as ardent in her faith as he? He was the one first seduced by the Quakers, but maybe after she was convinced she became the most fiery. Maybe it was she who said they would have to move to West Jersey for the sake of religious freedom. We'll never know. I just have to surmise that they shared a burning faith which was the very core of their lives and their marriage. How else could they endure all that they went through? Losing their babies, the uncertainty, the privations and then all those mosquitoes in South Jersey."

Harriet laughed. "I remember you talking about those mosquitoes," she said. "Faith, the water's boiling."

Faith poured the hot water into a cup, added instant coffee and stirred, then poured in a little milk. She took the cup carefully to her seat by the window. The pain was ebbing, but it was not quite gone. She debated taking a pill, and decided to wait for a bit.

"Well, that generation was certainly hardier than ours. Dad used to take us down to Cumberland to visit an old aunt of his every summer, and then out to see the old family homestead. We could hardly stand it, all those clouds of giant mosquitoes. But Martha and Joseph must have lived with them, with no screens and no repellent. Just accepted them as a normal part of life."

"I think I went with thee once," Harriet recalled. "A beautiful old brick farm house? And acres and acres of salt flats with that lovely marsh grass with the purple plumes."

"Acres and acres of salt flats," Faith agreed. "According to this copy of the deed he bought four hundred acres from the local Indians and six hundred more from other settlers when he began to prosper. But I was never sure how much of it was fast land and how much salt marsh. Anyway, it bred those truly gigantic mosquitoes."

"Perhaps a small price to pay for prosperity and religious freedom?" Harriet queried.

They were interrupted by the ringing of the phone. Although they had accepted its presence as a necessity, it still seemed like an intrusion into the silence of the cabin by the river, and its ring always startled them a little. The calls were usually for Faith, but this time she stayed in her seat by the window, wary of her back, and let Harriet pick up phone.

"It's for you," Harriet said. "Some young man. Shall I bring the phone over to you?"

"Please."

"Grandmere? Grandmere, it's Charlie. I'm in Philadelphia and I wondered if I could come out and see thee this afternoon? I've got my motorcycle."

"I'd love to have thee come," Faith said. "Can thee come for lunch? Or better yet, stay for dinner and spend the night?"

"No, I've got to get back to New York," Charlie said. "I didn't even know thee was living at Swallow Creek until I called Uncle David. That's how well my parents keep me informed."

"I think it is sometimes hard for thy parents to know exactly where thee is," Faith said, remembering the fear in Lucy's voice at time of the Democratic National Convention. "Well, come as soon as thee can for as long as thee can. I haven't had a proper visit with thee for years."

She hung up the phone thoughtfully. She hadn't seen Charlie since last Christmas, before her operation. He had seemed brooding and sullen, playing practically no part in the family festivities. The tension between him and his father, Bert, were tangible, surfacing over the dinner table in a few sharp words. Faith tried to reach out to him, but he was shut away from them all. A month later he called his parents to say he was dropping out of Columbia and moving to Brooklyn. He would drive a cab for bread money. Bert went down to talk with him, but was not able to persuade him to return to his classes. Bert returned to Cambridge and reported to Lucy that Charlie was living in a commune with a bunch of radicals. Lucy called Faith about this on the very day Faith learned she needed another operation. Lucy was tearful, and Faith felt unable to comfort her, or to know what to say. "Call me back tomorrow," she urged Lucy.

By the next day, Lucy had heard from Margaret and David about Faith's recurrence of cancer, and she wouldn't speak about Charlie when Faith called. The others changed the subject when she inquired about him. "Let's not worry mother," they must have agreed. Later, though, when she was in the hospital recovering from the operation she had received a letter from Charlie, not saying much about his present life, but expressing his love and concern for her, and mentioning the fun they had canoeing together when he came to stay with her on the river one summer while his parents were in Europe.

"It's my grandson, Charlie, he's coming out this afternoon," Faith said. "I do wonder if I have anything to say to him. Anything helpful, that is."

Harriet looked blank.

"He's our radical," Faith explained. "Which is all right with me, but not his parents, his father, especially. Unfortunately, Charlie is angry and unhappy. He's Lucy's eldest, and I think he's borne the brunt of a lot of trouble in that family. He used to seem like a quiet, steady boy, but he was always hard for them to reach."

"O dear, I hope he won't upset you," Harriet worried. "It isn't fair."

"Please, dearie, don't try to protect me," Faith said. "I want to be upset if that's what it takes to reach out to my grandchildren. It's part of being alive."

Harriet flushed. Faith had not meant to bring death into the room. "I think I'm going to take a little nap now, and be ready for Charlie," she said. "Don't worry about lunch; I'll grab something when I wake up." She was going to take one of those pills and see if she couldn't get rid of the pain in her back before Charlie arrived.

She had always had the gift of falling asleep easily, and now with the pill to help she quickly sank into a deep and restful oblivion. When she awoke she had trouble for a few seconds getting her bearings. There were voices from beyond her bedroom wall. She sat up carefully, but the pain seemed to be quite gone.

"O dear, I'm afraid I slept too long," she said, coming into the main room. Harriet was sitting at the table with a bearded stranger. It took Faith a moment to see it was Charlie with long hair and a glorious black beard. He wore blue jeans and a torn leather jacket. A motorcycle helmet sat on the table next to him. The remains of lunch were on the table.

"Thee's just in time for some chicken soup." Harriet said.

"She spoils me," Faith said, going up to Charlie and bending over to give him a hug. He smelled a little over-ripe, and his beard tickled, but his smile was warm and unguarded, and she caught a glimpse of him as a little boy, so many years ago.

"How is thee, grandmere?" he asked, getting to his feet. Proper manners had been taught in the Levering household, and were probably hard to shake.

"I'm really surprisingly well," Faith said. "Sit, down, Charlie. Tell us what brings thee to Philadelphia?"

Harriet got up and bustled about, getting Faith's lunch. Faith wished she wouldn't do this, but decided not to say anything with Charlie there.

"I came down to attend a meeting," Charlie said. "We have to decide on a new strategy after Chicago. Did thee know I go arrested?"

46

"Yes, I heard," Faith said. She remembered Lucy's tearful voice over the phone at midnight. "Bert is so angry he's thinking of writing a letter stating that he will pay no more of Charlie's bills until we get a full apology for this."

"Grandmere, it was awful, all those angry faced pigs beating up on the marchers. Taking out their rage on us."

"It looked pretty violent on TV," Faith said. "Of course they did show some of the marchers taunting the police."

"The media looks for stuff like that," Charlie said. "They are in the pay of the bosses, like everyone else in the system."

"But didn't a camera man get beaten as well?" Faith asked.

"O well, exceptions, of course," Charlie said.

Harriet brought her a bowl of soup and a cheese sandwich and she began to eat. She discovered that she was actually quite hungry.

"So did you decide on a new strategy?" she asked Charlie. "Or is that a secret?"

"O, more organizing, more efforts to recruit workers into antiwar actions," Charlie said. "It probably won't work with the way this country is going fascist. Pretty soon we'll have Tricky Dick for president, and then he'll declare all protest is illegal, or something."

"You are sure he is going to win?"

"Well, he doesn't have any good opposition. And I'd rather have him than Humphrey. After what he did in Chicago, Humphrey doesn't deserve a single vote," Charlie said.

Harriet and Faith exchanged a quick glance. They intended to return to Philadelphia next week to vote, and they had confessed to each other they were going to vote for Humphrey, though Faith had some reservations.

"Thee isn't going to vote for that man, is thee grandmere?" Charlie asked, catching the exchange.

"What's the alternative?" Faith asked. "I don't want Nixon. Thee is too little to remember the fifties, but he was about as bad as Joseph McCarthy."

"Thee could vote for Dick Gregory," Charlie suggested. "But some people say even if Nixon gets in he's more apt to get us out of this war than Humphrey. Nixon is an opportunist; he'll listen to the voice of the people if he thinks it will help his career."

"Hmm, I wonder about that," Faith said. "But this war must end; it's tearing up our own society as well as destroying that of the Vietnamese."

"Gee, grandmere, it's good to hear thee say that," Charlie said. "My father is still on the kick about the domino theory, believe it or not. If Vietnam falls to communism, we'll be next. And mother just looks unhappy and says nothing. She was raised a Quaker, wasn't she? You'd think she'd at least be willing to stand up to him about the war."

"Thy father is immersed in the law," Faith said. "And he has a very logical mind. A logical argument can be made for the pacifist position, but ultimately it rests on something else, a faith in the Holy Spirit working through the human race."

"You don't have to be a religious pacifist to be against this war," Charlie pointed out. "Colleagues of his right at Harvard Law School disagree with him."

"Well, it is all very difficult," Faith said. "But let's not worry about it right now, shall we? I was hoping thee could take time for a short paddle downstream with me. We can go right away and I'll do the dishes later."

"Should thee paddle?" Charlie asked, looking from Faith to Harriet and back again.

"Yes, I'm allowed," Faith said. "I'm allowed to do anything I feel like doing this year." The pain in her back had returned a little but it was dulled by the pills. She was sure she could make it at least part way down the river and back.

"I'll do the dishes," Harriet said. "There are hardly any, anyway. Now scoot."

"Let's go then," Charlie said. He grinned, and Faith saw again a glimpse of the shy, sweet boy she had known, behind the massive black beard. She allowed him to take her elbow and help her down the steps to the dock, and watched with pleasure the skill with which he swung the canoe around against the current and held it steady for her to get in.

They canoed in silence for some time, their paddles dipping in unison into the still surface of the water. Once, rounding a curve, they startled a flight of ducks. American mergansers, Faith thought, as they rose before them. After a time they stopped to rest at a dockside.

"I've been thinking a lot about privilege," Faith said. "Is it really fair, that we own all this wonderful land and silence, while the migrant workers who pick the blueberries in the fields around here can't even swim in the stream?"

"Well, true," Charlie said. "But compared to the sort of privilege that exists in this country right now, I'd say thine is pretty austere."

"Yes, but it blinds us," Faith said. "It confuses us. Did thee ever read John Woolman's journal? When he told us that we ought to look to our possessions, the furniture of our houses, and see if they contained the seeds of war?"

"They never taught us much Quakerism at home," Charlie said. "That's good though. Seeds of war. Sounds like the old boy was a proto socialist."

"Well, not exactly, " Faith said. "He wanted more than anything else in the world to be open to the Holy Spirit. He wanted us to get rid of war and slavery so we could be closer to God."

"Sounds like a rationalization for seeking justice." Charlie said.

"Not if you believed that men and women could be instruments of the Holy Spirit in building a peaceful kingdom," Faith said. "In that case, being close to God is the best way to seek justice."

"Pretty hard to believe all that any more," Charlie said, "when you see what people are willing to do to one another. Woolman wouldn't have lasted long in Chicago."

"Maybe or maybe not," Faith said. "It's what Martin Luther King was all about, wasn't it? And I sometimes think there is a sort of blind hunger for that kind of faith today."

"Yes, well, maybe I ought to read Woolman," Charlie said. "If I ever get time to read again. Maybe in jail."

"Is thee going to jail?" Faith asked.

"Well, I'm not going to Vietnam and I'm not going to Canada," Charlie said. "Mother wants me to claim to be a conscientious objector, but I'm really not. So what else is there?"

"I've just been reading about an ancestor of thine and mine who went to jail," Faith told him.

"For resisting the draft?" Charlie asked.

"No, for being a Quaker," Faith said. "It was in Massachusetts in the seventeenth century. And later he was expelled and had to travel overland. So it was a faith worth everything to him, too."

Charlie was quiet, and they sat still in the canoe, watching the clear water dimple and swirl past. Did Martha and Joseph pass this river on their way overland to Cumberland, Faith wondered? Did they encounter the Lenni Lenape, who once lived here? Were they afraid of the Indians, despite their faith in that of God in everyone? There was so much she would never know. Only that they had faith, a depth of faith she could hardly conceive of, despite her name. How could she begin to describe it to this troubled but searching grandson whose greatest need, she saw, was to have more faith in himself?

"Mother never told me a thing about her ancestors," Charlie said. "And gran, I don't remember that thee did, either."

"I didn't," Faith admitted. "I'm only just beginning to be interested and see connections. But Charlie? I think we better start back now."

The pain in her back had arisen again, and was coiled like a snake up and down her backbone. She began to long for one of the little green pills on her bedroom bureau.

Charlie swung the canoe about, and they started upstream, fighting the current. Faith only paddled at the curves, and between times sat back, hoping to ease the pain. There was still so much she ought to say to Charlie, and yet the pain was there like an enemy, distracting her thoughts. How was she to complete this year with such an adversary? "O Martha, be with me," she thought. "Lend me thy strength this winter."

Chapter 5

NOVEMBER 15, 1968

By mid November, the last leaves had fallen, and a new landscape had emerged along the banks of Swallow Creek. It was, Faith noted, a surprisingly colorful landscape. Evergreens, hidden by the summer foliage, were suddenly vivid in the barren woods; sheep laurel and mountain laurel, swamp magnolia and ground pine, jack pine and cedar, all stood forth in shades of green. The pink tipped high blueberry bushes added rose and taupe in the view from her window; the fallen bracken, soft golds and browns; the grasses, mauves and ambers.

"I always thought November was a dreary month, but down here I discover it is brilliant," she told Harriet.

"It's the quality of the light," Harriet said.

Faith was spending more time now sitting by the window. The day after Charlie's visit she had called Frank Stoddard to tell him about the new pain, and he had set up appointments for a series of tests. Fortunately the cancer hadn't spread to her backbone, as she had feared. The pain she was experiencing was reflected from the tumor growing in her intestinal tract. Frank gave her a new and slightly stronger course of chemotherapy, and a bottle of pain killers which she was to take every four hours, whether or not the pain was there.

"But I don't want to feel woozy," Faith objected. "I want my wits about me."

"These pills are really mild," Frank told her. "You'll scarcely feel them, and this way, you can keep ahead of the pain."

Faith was a bit skeptical, but the pills seemed to work, and she was content to sit quietly for hours, reading her family papers, or knitting. She and Harriet were settling into an ever more comfortable pattern of life together. Harriet was beginning to lose her tendency to fuss over Faith, and to accept Faith's occasional bad mornings without an attack of anxiety. She allowed Faith to do some of the cooking, and no longer followed, like a small worried terrier, when Faith felt like taking a short walk along the river. More and more, they were learning to share silences as well as conversation.

On Fridays, Harriet drove to Mt. Ephraim to shop at the large supermarket, and to fill Faith's prescriptions at the apothecary's. If they ran out of things in between times they could drive to the Paxtons, the neat-as-a-pin local store. White haired Mr. Paxton and his wife had served as caretakers for the cabins along Swallow Creek for the past forty years, earning a stipend from the association. They knew all the old families along the river, and could furnish details about who was in poor health, or had a new grand-child or had been down recently for a long weekend.

"Our needs are not just answered, they are antici-
pated," Faith wrote Anne. "Margaret and David come
down regularly, and Margaret is always looking around for
something we might need and having it delivered the next
day. We aren't just cared for, we are coddled."

Faith's flow of visitors continued to be phenomenal.
The Terrills, a charming couple from New Hope with
whom she had worked for the AFSC in Algeria, came down
to visit, as well as Frieda Richards, a friend from the earliest overseas mission in Grand Pre. There were visitors
from Haverford, and from the Spring Street settlement
house, on the board of which she still served. Sylvia
Shipley, with whom she had gone to Westtown, came
often from nearby Mt. Ephraim. Fortunately Harriet had
a good many visitors too, so there was no painful discrep-
ancy. And they were beginning to make friends with their
neighbors along the river.

Faith was not alone in having converted her cabin for
winter use. A retired professor from New York University
and his social worker wife had bought the old Lewis place
downstream and fixed it up for year round living. Ben and
Lillian Stroman called soon after Faith and Harriet
moved in and Faith liked them well enough. They had the
enthusiasm of city dwellers newly converted to country
living for every plant, every bird, every small animal along
the river. Unfortunately they were both extremely talka-
tive, interrupting each other in their enthusiasm to tell
the little tales of their daily life, with their voices still
pitched to the decibels of the city. Faith suspected that
they might be a little lonely, missing the stimulation of

city life, despite their vigorous denials. She tried to be cordial, but she could feel a wall of Philadelphia reserve freezing around her. She felt she might not be able to deal with too many visits from the Stromans in the course of the winter.

The talk turned to the recent election. The Stromans had voted for Dick Gregory as a protest, they said, against Hubert Humphrey's betrayal at the Chicago convention. They were however heartsick about the election of Richard Nixon.

"At least down here we don't have to watch what is going to happen to the inner cities," Lillian Stroman said.

"Why didn't thee tell them that thee had lived in New York when Tom taught at Columbia?" Harriet asked after the Stromans had finally left. "And all that work thee did at Hudson Guild? She worked at a settlement house too; she probably knows lots of people that thee knew."

"I thought perhaps I'd wait to bring that up until we know them a little better," Faith said cautiously. "Sometimes mutual friends can be too much of a good thing."

Upstream were the young Platts. Donald Platt had taught biology at Haverford College for years and was one of Tom's oldest friends. When Elsie Platt heard that Faith was moving down to the river she had come to tell her about young Don and his wife and baby. Halfway through a graduate program at MIT the boy had announced he was abandoning the pursuit of knowledge to become a carpenter and to live simply and in harmony with nature. He and his wife Susie had joined a communal group in

Vermont for a while, but it hadn't worked out. When Susie got pregnant they wanted to settle somewhere else, and Elsie had hit on the idea of offering them the cabin at Swallow Creek.

"After all, no one in the family uses it any more," Elsie had said apologetically to Faith. "And I don't suppose that they'll do anything that's too offensive to the other families. At least, I hope not." She sighed. "My sister thinks I shouldn't be subsidizing them in this fashion. If they didn't have a nice place to live they might come to their senses and Don go back to school. But it might be worse. They might join another commune, or get involved with a cult, or something. It is hard to know what is right."

"I think thee has done the right thing," Faith told her. "They'll be nice neighbors. And if it shakes up a few of our stuffier members, then it will be good for them. Force them to think a little."

Uncertain perhaps of their welcome at the Smedley camp, the young Platts kept to themselves at first, and only waved as they paddled past, their baby a tiny bundle in a bright blue life jacket.

"Let's paddle downstream and see them this afternoon," Faith suggested one bright, warm November morning.

Harriet agreed, and after lunch they set forth. Getting off the dock Faith misjudged her footing, and for a moment the canoe wobbled wildly. She sat down heavily, clutching the sides and staring down into the water until her heart stopped hammering. It would be very cold now.

If she did fall in, would the queasy feeling in her stomach sharpen to pain? Would she be able to swim to shore?

"When Jack and Kate come down next weekend I think we ought to let them put away the canoe," Harriet said. "I really did promise my children we would stop canoeing in November."

"Agreed," Faith said.

Once out on the river, they found it was not quite as warm as it had seemed. A sharp wind blew across the pine barrens, rippled the water, and found chinks and crannies in their jackets. They paddled briskly to keep warm. Rounding a curve they came to a place where the river had recently shifted its bed, leaving a quiet backwater full of water lilies in summer. From the surface of this pond a flight of ducks rose at their approach, a series of whirring explosions as they shot from the water.

"Black ducks? Or mallards?" Harriet asked hopefully.

"I'm afraid just mallards," Faith said.

At the Platt dock a bearded young giant met them and helped them carefully one by one from their canoe. "I'm glad you came," he said, after they had introduced themselves. His light brown hair was clubbed back, and his beard trimmed. Faith found him handsome and wondered if he might look something like the Quakers of Joseph White's day.

"It's good to see you, Don," Faith said. "It's been many years."

In the cabin keeping room, where he took them, a steamy chaos reigned. Susie Platt was boiling a pail of diapers and baking bread at the same time, moving between the old fashioned wood stove and a work table with deft bare feet, and managing to avoid stepping on the baby who played on the floor, along with a puppy, weaving in and out of bags of groceries and trash. Don introduced her proudly as she came forward to greet her guests, wiping her hands on her bluejeans, a tall, loose limbed girl with straight blonde hair parted in the middle and hanging down her back, her unbound breasts heavy with milk swinging under a torn tee shirt.

"We're in kind of a mess," she said, clearing off a load of laundry from one kitchen chair for Faith, and another for Harriet, and dumping the clothes onto a bed in the corner of the room. "Don has a day off and he's trying to get some insulation in." She pointed to a wall of the room where pink sheets of insulation were tacked between the uprights.

"Don't apologize." Faith could see that Don didn't like it. After all, this was the life style they had chosen, and in which they believed. She sat down a trifle heavily in the proffered chair and peeked at the baby under the table. A little girl, about a year old, her bright blue eyes met Faith's eagerly and she smiled.

"Where do you get your whole wheat flour?" Harriet asked Susie, seeing the bag on the table.

"We still drive to Philadelphia to the food co-op," Susie said. "Everything natural they sell. We can get it at the Haddonfield one, but we are afraid it doesn't move as rapidly and may develop molds."

She fixed them sassafras tea served in pottery mugs as they talked about diet. The Platts were vegetarians, they said. They baked their own bread, cultured their own yogurt, got whole raw goat milk from a local farmer. They composted their garbage, and with it had last summer actually grown vegetables in the New Jersey sand behind the cabin. They had tried canning their excess produce but it hadn't worked too well; some of the food had gone bad. In the spring Don was going to build an electric freezer so they could freeze vegetables as well as the wild blueberries which grew in profusion along the stream. The only thing was, the freezer would use electricity. They were thinking about ways to generate their own power from the swift current of the stream.

Faith was fascinated. Anne had written that her son Jim, who had joined an Eastern religious group, had some of the same ideas, but she had never had a chance to talk to Jim about it. She asked sympathetic questions, until Don finally dropped his reserve and began to explain the implications he saw in this; a whole new society growing up parallel to the crumbling world order; a society based on frugality, sharing and joy.

While they talked the baby crawled out from under the table, climbed onto her mother's lap, and tugged at her tee shirt, until Susie unselfconsciously nursed her. The bread began to smell delicious. Don got up and tested it, then slipped it back for a few minutes more.

"I was in a women's group in Cambridge," Susie said. "Don and I try to share tasks on an equal basis. Only right now he needs to go out and earn the money, and I'm lucky enough to be able to stay here and play with Debby and work on my weaving." She indicated a large loom at one corner of the room.

Satisfied at last, the baby climbed down, and came over to Faith. She stood at her knee a moment, then evidently convinced it was safe, climbed up into Faith's lap. Her diapers, Faith discovered were not only damp, but apparently loaded. The odor was reminiscent and not unpleasant, not unlike that of the baking bread.

"How is thee?" Faith asked the baby seriously. "I feel that we are going to be friends."

When it was time to leave, Don lent Faith a copy of the *Whole Earth Catalogue*. "You really should try their herbal remedies," he told her earnestly. "There have been many cures."

So Elsie must have written them about Faith's illness.

"I'll read it," she said. "I'm perfectly willing to try anything. But you must come down and visit us, and bring Debby."

"And if we can ever take you to Mt. Ephraim to shop, let us know," Harriet added. "Or just up to Paxtons, for that matter."

The Platts glanced at each other. "We never go to Paxtons," Don said tersely, back to his earlier brusqueness.

"Why not?" Faith was startled.

"Because we don't like their politics," Don said.

"They won't deal with anyone but Anglo-Saxons," Susie explained, seeing Faith's confusion. "The Costas have to go all the way to Mt. Ephraim even if they just need a bottle of milk."

"And in the summer, when the migrants are here picking blueberries he keeps a gun under the counter in case any of them come near the store," Don added bitterly.

Faith was stunned. "Did thee know that?" she asked Harriet.

"Well, I knew Angelina never went there," Harriet said tentatively. "But I wasn't sure why."

" Good Lord," Faith said. " And I went carting off to Algeria to help right the wrongs of imperialism. It just goes to show one can support injustice in all innocence."

Don Platt smiled.

"I guess you think people like us guard our innocence," Faith said shrewdly.

"O, I'm sure that Don didn't mean that," Susie said, and blushed. Clearly, boarding school manners were proving hard to shed.

"No one around here will sell or rent to migrants," Don Platt continued, speaking mildly. "The Costas have a nephew, Stephen, who is their only relative in the States. Stephen works in Mt. Ephraim but has to live in Camden and commute."

On the way home, Faith and Harriet were silent. The wind had freshened, and now buffeted their light canoe. They were going against the current, and needed to paddle hard in order to keep in midstream. Faith found her heart pounding, and she acknowledged she was a little frightened. What was she, a seriously ill woman of seventy-six, doing out here, leading Harriet like a faithful Sancho into danger? They must definitely have the canoe put away next weekend. No more paddling until spring. And then? Her heart lurched. I'm not ready to give up, she admitted to herself. Not all this. Already at four the sun was beginning to set, and the somber autumnal colors to deepen and glow. A bare giant tree with twisted limbs, like an Arthur Rackham fantasy, loomed ahead, its branches black against the brilliant sky. "Long have I known a splendor in it all, but never knew I this," she whispered to herself.

The conversation with the young Platts returned to haunt her as soon as they had safely brought the canoe to their dock and climbed to their cabin.

"The Paxtons are my responsibility," she told Harriet over their simple supper. "In addition to the work he does for the association, he watches over certain of the cabins. Dad paid him a sum every month, and I'm sure my lawyer still does. The Quaker community has subsidized him for years. I'm going to have to speak to him about this."

"Doesn't thee think the association ought to do it?" Harriet asked anxiously. "They might not all agree with thee."

"I'll bring it up at the next meeting," Faith said, "but in addition I think I ought to say something about the Costas. I feel a concern, as my ancestors would have said."

In the morning she dressed carefully. At the store she found both husband and wife behind the counter. She dawdled over her purchases until the lone customer had left, before approaching the couple. They greeted her enthusiastically. They had known her all their lives as the White girl, although she was actually ten years older than they. Now they were eager to catch up on the news of the Philadelphia families whom they had known as Swallow Creek residents. Was it true that the older Evans girl was getting a divorce? Had anyone told her about the wild party that young Peter Warrington had had at his family's camp last summer? Was someone finally going to buy the Satterthwaite place? It was such a shame, they thought that so few families came down any more.

"Well, it looks like some of them are going to recolonize," Faith said. "I'm here and we visited the young Platts yesterday."

Mr. Paxton looked down, frowned, and began to wipe the counter top.

"One of the ladies at our church asked me who those hippies are," Mrs. Paxton said, giggling, and patting her smoothly waved hair. "I know he's supposed to be a college graduate and all, but with that beard and long hair he sure looks like a hippy to me."

Faith felt her face flush. One battle at a time, she told herself.

"By the way, you know Angelina Costa is working for me this winter," she said easily. "It would be convenient for her to do her shopping here from time to time."

"If she is shopping for you, Mrs. Smedley, of course it will be all right," Mrs. Paxton said.

Her husband shot her a glance. "We are required by law to serve everybody," he said brusquely.

"Yes, but there are ways of making people feel welcome or unwelcome," Faith ventured.

"I tell you, Mrs. Smedley, it's the ones who come in the summer." Mr. Paxton leaned over the counter, seeking to take her into his confidence. "Maybe it's not their fault, poor devils, but the way they live is something to behold. Well, the truth is, Mrs. Smedley, they aren't too clean. And half the time by evening when they are through work and want to shop they've had a couple of beers. We just can't have them around the store, Mrs. Smedley. I've got you people down along the river to think about. What if they started using that beach up the river next to you? You wouldn't want your children swimming in the same water. If I didn't keep them off that beach they'd be washing their clothes and God knows what else up stream from you. For thirty years I've kept that element off the river, and I know the association wants me to continue."

Faith looked at him quizzically, and he misunderstood. "Oh not just me, alone, Mrs. Smedley. I don't want to take credit away from the sheriff. The sheriff does a lot. He's in and out of there twice a week, three times a week in the summer. He's flushed a lot of undesirables out of your woods. He does his duty by you, no mistake. But I help him, and let him know if there's someone about that looks suspicious. Not a cabin broken into for the past four years. Think of that."

"You can't let a lot of empty properties sit around down here and not protect it," Mrs. Paxton added virtuously. "Down here there's just one thing that the people understand and that's the strong arm of the law. Fire power."

Faith flinched. "It's a paradox, a Quaker community defended by fire power," she said.

Mr. Paxton flushed and ran his hand nervously over his balding head. "Some people, for all their money and their brains, don't know much," he said mysteriously. "Some people are full of pious thoughts, but they go off and leave the working people, like me and Mary here, to do the dirty work. Never an extra penny for a picture show, while some people are off to Maine or Florida or Europe or heaven knows where, too busy even to come down once a year and check on their own property."

Faith flushed, and willed her heart to stop beating so wildly. Words of defense rose to her lips, but what he said, she recognized, was true. Probably the association paid the Paxtons miserably for their caretaking. Quakers were always frugal. She must look into it.

"We do appreciate all you do for us," she finally said when she knew she could keep her voice light, "and I know it must be hard. But I feel personally I cannot buy my groceries here anymore unless the Costas can. I hope you'll let them. We've been coming here for years."

They were quiet a moment. A drowsy fly buzzed at the window, otherwise the little store was suddenly still. "If there is that of God in everyone I ought to know how to speak to that of God in Friend Paxton," Faith thought. "But I don't seem to know how."

Mr. Paxton turned to his cash register and began to ring up Faith's purchases, stabbing the keys viciously. Mrs. Paxton looked at him, then turned and walked straight to the door that led from the store to their living quarters.

"There you are, Mrs. Smedley," he said briskly. "That will be $6.71. Tell the Costas they are welcome at any time, but I don't want them bringing friends with them next summer."

He handed her the sack of groceries and she paid him, and walked away, feeling bewildered and sick at heart.

Chapter 6

NOVEMBER 28, 1968

The Smedley Thanksgiving was to be held at David and Margaret's home in Chestnut Hill. In her first flush of enthusiasm for life on Swallow Creek, Faith had proposed to her children that they come there for the family gathering, but Margaret had been quick to rule that idea out. There wouldn't be room to seat all seventeen, let alone deal with a turkey in Faith's small oven.

"Seventeen?" Faith queried. "Does thee mean Anne and Roger are coming?"

"Coming and bringing their whole tribe," Margaret announced triumphantly. "Including young Paul's new wife. I asked Aunt Jane and Uncle Harry, but they are both having their own children to dinner. They'll come by to see thee the next day."

"How wonderful," Faith said. She had a sudden awareness of the telephone conversations that must have taken place. *But you must come. It will be her last Thanksgiving. What about Christmas instead? I don't think we had better put it off. She's still in remission but we don't know how she'll be by Christmas time. Maybe okay but maybe not.*

"Margaret means well," Faith told Harriet, "But I really don't like to feel so managed. Especially at this stage in my life."

"Well, I'm going to feel better about it," Harriet said cautiously. "I don't really much want to leave you here alone, even for a night, but I must go to the family party at Christopher's."

"What I hate is to leave the river, even for a day," Faith confessed. "It keeps changing so, I'm afraid I'll miss something."

It was true, every day brought variations to the colors of late fall; more purples and browns, less gold, more mauve. Several mornings now they had awakened to see hoar frost glittering on the grasses and tiny tendrils of steam rising from the water. Faith was finding that she could just sit and stare at the flow of the river for long stretches of time. There was deep thirst within her for the peace and serenity, the spiritual nurture, of the scene. She felt sometimes as though she had been rushing pell mell though life toward some unimagined end. She needed now to store her energies for the final spurt.

"I never thought of thee as a homebody," David told her Wednesday night, driving her to Philadelphia, and hearing about her reluctance to leave Swallow Creek. "After all, thee has led a rather nomadic life, hasn't thee?"

"It's a new development," Faith told him. "I'm having an identity crisis at seventy-six."

Nevertheless, it was pleasant to arrive at the big house on West Moreland, smell the lemony furniture oil, see the flowers, and sink into a comfortable chair in the living room. There was something to be said for the amenities after all, she observed, especially when your bones continually ached, and you felt a bit queasy inside.

Peggy and Tim were already home for the holidays, Peggy having come down from New York on a crowded afternoon train, and Tim having gotten a ride down from Cambridge with a housemate. There were just five of them for supper, and Margaret set up a small table before the living room fire and served a simple but delicious meal; a seafood casserole, green beans and a salad. Faith wasn't very hungry, but she tried to eat small amounts of everything to keep her state to herself. Once she caught Peggy watching her. No use arousing additional anxieties. They were drinking coffee when Lucy and Bert arrived, with three of their children, having eaten on the road.

"Mother, thee looks wonderful, so relaxed and brown," Lucy said, after embracing her. "I think I ought to spend a year on Swallow Creek too."

"I think thee'd love it," Faith said. She thought Lucy did indeed look as though she could benefit from some extra rest. She was thinner than she was last summer, and there was a look of added tension about her eyes and mouth. Perhaps they were having a marital crisis again, Faith thought. But then, Lucy had always looked tense. At forty-seven she had managed to acquire almost as many gray hairs as Faith at seventy-six. I've always worried about her, Faith told herself, and the poor girl shows it, that's all.

Bert, shaking hands with David and Tim, looked, on the contrary, in the pink. He was one of those large blonde men who seldom show age, and he kept after himself; playing tennis in season and out, jogging in the early mornings. There was a look of animal vitality about him that might make him a demanding husband. Could it be that a child of hers, that Lucy, could be unresponsive? Faith wondered.

The three Levering girls followed their parents into the house, lugging suitcases and the living room exploded into a melee of greetings. Faith, urged to stay seated in her big chair was kissed cautiously by Jennifer and Barbara and hugged by young Susan. Faith's heart raced a little anxiously. I'm not used to crowds any more, she thought.

"Grandmere?" Jennifer knelt at her feet, looking like a portrait of one of her Quaker ancestors with her granny glasses and her hair pulled back into a bun. "Grandmere, I met a woman who used to know thee ages ago. Her husband teaches economics at Harvard and she came to my women's group to tell us about the suffragists. Her name is Virginia Bloom and she says she and her husband worked in the West Virginia coal fields when thee and grandfather were in charge of self-help."

"O Virginia!" Faith exclaimed, warmed by the thought of her old friend. "I haven't seen her in ages. Give her my best love. But darling, Virginia was too young to be a suffragist."

"Yes, but she says her mother was. She's reading her mother's journal and writing a book about it."

Faith laughed. "As a matter of fact I remember vividly one night when Marshall Bloom stalked into the kitchen shouting, 'Why isn't my dinner on the table?' And Virginia, who was about twice his size, scurrying about to make it."

Jennifer looked horrified. "But she seemed so liberated. He must have been a real chauvinist."

"Just a little man who needed to prove himself," Faith said. "I have the impression he came from a family where that mattered."

"Didn't it matter in all families?" Jennifer asked. "I mean in those days? Except maybe for Quakers?"

"Quakers weren't always exempt," Faith told her. "Fortunately thy grandfather had been raised to share in the housework." She ought to tred delicately, she thought. Jennifer's father had some pretty definite ideas about the respect due the male.

Jennifer laughed. "We had a boy at our workcamp last summer who was taught to think women should do all the work," she said. "He didn't even know how to boil an egg. By the end of the summer we had him cooking dinner for the sixteen of us."

"Thee hasn't told me much about thy workcamp," Faith said.

"The workcamp was fine, but next summer I'm going to find an all women's group. Thee wasn't a suffragist, was thee?" Jennifer asked.

"I didn't know much about it," Faith confessed, "I was too busy playing field hockey in college. And then I married your grandfather and went overseas."

"I didn't know thee played field hockey, grandmere," Barbara said. She had been standing nearby, listening, waiting for her turn to speak to Faith. "Which position?"

"Left wing," Faith said. "I hear thee made all star. I'd love to come and see thee play."

Barbara's eyes lit up. She was a blonde and stocky girl, a female replica of her father. Like him, she was more interested in sports than causes. "Do come, grandmere. Come next fall when we play thy old school, Wellesley," she said. Jennifer looked at her and she blushed. "Or come this spring and see the lacrosse game with Smith."

"Did you know that grandmere was all star too?" Jennifer asked her sister.

"Of course I knew," Barbara said crossly. The two girls, close in age, were miles apart in every possible way. Susie, the youngest was still in high school, a stocky brown haired girl, an athlete like Barbara, but quiet as Charlie had been.

"Where's Charlie?" Faith asked

"Who knows?" Jennifer laughed. "Mother left a message for him, and we hope he'll show up sometime tomorrow."

"He'll come," Susie said with conviction. "He'll come to see grandmere." Faith saw that the child's brown eyes were swimming with tears. Lucy shouldn't have told the children, she thought. But of course that wasn't the modern way. Everything had to be out in the open. Well, it was hard to know what was right.

"That was mean of me to tell that story on Marshall Bloom," she said to Jennifer. "He is a fine man, and we all have some skeletons in our closets."

The Leverings finished unloading the car while David fussed over the fire. When they were reassembled, Margaret brought cups of hot mulled cider. Faith, beginning to feel better, looked around at the large bodies draped here and there about the living room. Two children and five grandchildren, the fruit of her womb, and of her love of Tom. Talk about the population explosion she thought wryly. And another six still to come. But they were good people, all of them, and perhaps one among them would do something worth while for the world.

In the middle of the night she awakened to the sounds of fresh arrivals. Anne and Roger Krueger had driven straight through from Indianapolis. Her heart jumped at the sound of her younger daughter's voice. How she had loved that child! She recognized Roger's deep base and her grandson, Paul, sounding like his father. Where in the world would Margaret put them all? She drifted back to sleep, still counting beds.

She awakened early, feeling wretched. Her head ached, and her stomach lurched with nausea. That seafood! She lay very still willing herself not to panic. She must not be sick, on this day of days. She watched the dawn creep into the room, awakening each object of furniture from the darkness of the night, until she felt strong enough to slip out of bed and get to her suitcase wherein lay the precious antinausea pills Frank had given her for such emergencies. Running water in the bathroom, she felt she might be going to throw up, but she managed to swallow the pill with only a sip of water, then creep back into bed and lie still until the blessed calm came. She dozed again, and awakened in broad daylight with a delightful sense of ease and well being. She was even a bit hungry.

She got up, dressed quietly, and crept downstairs, intending to get herself some tea and toast. Passing the living room she saw the solution to the bedding problem.

There were four large bodies in sleeping bags distributed about the living room rug. Margaret would surely not be enthusiastic about this arrangement, being a tidy house-keeper. Yes, but she had probably planned it this way in order to get everyone into the house for Faith's last Thanksgiving. Thee might be a little more charitable, she told herself sternly.

In the kitchen she found Margaret herself, already at work stuffing a large turkey. She wanted to help, but the bird did not look appetizing with its pale skin glistening with grease, and she was glad when Margaret insisted that she have her tea first. She was just finishing when Lucy arrived, hoping to help fix breakfast, followed by Anne. At forty-six, Anne still wore her hair in a page boy cut she had worn in high school, and it looked almost the same, hardly touched with gray. Faith hadn't seen her since her operation last spring, and she found tears welling up in her eyes when she embraced her. She was still the same sturdy, happy faced girl she had been so many years ago.

"With three of us at work there really isn't anything for thee to do but cheer us on," Margaret said, and Faith agreed. After David came down she took a second cup of tea into the dining room and sat at the big table, as one by one the members of her family drifted in for breakfast.

Paul, the Krueger's oldest child, had left graduate school last year, gotten married and joined an Eastern religious sect. They lived communally, and had a guru, who visited them from time to time from India. Faith didn't know much about it, and made a mental note to try to talk to him sometime. Paul had grown his hair long, and a pale, rather wispy beard sprouted from his chin, but he looked much happier than when Faith had seen him last. Ellen, the new wife, was plump and dark and unexpectedly vivid. Paul was obviously bursting with pride in her; he brought her to Faith and watched happily as Ellen bent to kiss her on the cheek. Faith was conscious of moist lips and a slight odor of unwashed clothes. The old tie up between cleanliness and Godliness was lost on these latter day saints, it seemed.

Beth Krueger came in shortly after her brother. She was a twenty-one year old art student who looked astonishingly like her mother, and Faith's heart had always gone out to her in a special way. It was reciprocated. Beth wrote her long, sprawling letters, sharing her moods and feelings in a way which Faith thought was quite remarkable. Beth had been living for almost a year with a former medical student who now worked as a carpenter for bread, as Beth put it, while he tried to decide what to do next. They weren't ready for marriage quite yet, Beth had written. Faith was deeply touched that Beth trusted her enough to tell her about this arrangement.

Now, entering the dining room, Beth paused at the sight of Faith, then went over to the sideboard, and was busy rearranging the flowers. "Hi, grandmere," she said softly, and Faith saw that she was fighting for control. Do I really look that bad? Faith wondered. How much more of this can I take? But that's not the question is it? How can I help them?

"Thee didn't bring thy special friend," she said. "Rich, is that his name?"

"He had to go home to his family," Beth said. "I'll bring him another time to meet you."

"Bring him down to Swallow Creek," Faith suggested. "Come in the spring when it begins to get warm."

"Anybody save any breakfast for me?" Dan asked, striding in, and planting an unselfconscious kiss on the top of Faith's head. Dan was a happy-go-lucky nineteen year old. He had refused to go to college at all, but was working as an auto mechanic at a garage in a small town near the Kruegers, saving all his money to buy a racing car. Anne and Roger had accepted his decision, as they had accepted Beth's going to art school, and Paul's turn to an Eastern religion, with what appeared to be a matter of fact naturalness.

"I'd like to go on having babies, just to see who each of them would turn out to be," Anne had once said to Faith. "I never expected Dan to be Dan." Faith admired this openness. In fact, she admired Anne and Roger as parents. They had never pursued the cocktail circuit as Lucy and Bert did, or devoted hours to good works in the community as David and Margaret did. Instead, Roger had deliberately chosen a form of group practice which gave him maximum time with his family. They lived on a farm outside of Indianapolis and had raised their children with an abundance of dogs, cats, horses and love. It had been a good marriage and a good family. All the relationships appeared solid. And yet the Krueger children seemed to be having a harder time than the Levering children finding their way. Was there a malaise of the young today that transcended individual family patterns?

As the grandchildren came and went, breakfast became a Mad Hatter's tea party, with many shifts in eating, and accumulating piles of dirty dishes. Dinner preparations went on in the kitchen in a rising crescendo of bustle and good odors. Faith was glad to sit and sip her herb tea and watch the interplay of strong personalities all around her.

Despite some surface similarities there was no love lost between first cousins Jennifer and Beth, she noticed. Born within a few months of each other, they had always been up for comparison within the family. It had evidently made them feel competitive from an early age. Was this because Lucy had always suspected that Anne was Faith's favorite daughter, she wondered? If she were responsible, it was too late for regrets.

Tim and Paul, on the other hand, although at opposite polls in their ideas, seemed to have an easy relationship between them. They talked about people they had known in common at Westtown or Pocono Lake Preserve, and rock music they enjoyed. With Paul, Tim let down his bland smooth guard a little.

Ellen, Paul's new wife had come in late, and was now in the kitchen, fixing a special vegetarian dish for Paul and herself, as well as Beth, who had become a vegetarian several years earlier.

"What about Charlie?" Beth asked. "Is he still eating meat?"

"Whenever he can get it," Jennifer said. "Steaks as a matter of fact."

"I can't understand how you can believe in social transformation and still eat meat," Paul said. "If everyone in the world were to have the same meal this Thanksgiving we would all have a bowl of rice, with a bit of sauce, a cup of tea and a thin slice of dark bread."

"Yes, but if I were to eat less today that doesn't mean that a starving child in Bangladesh is going to eat more," Peggy pointed out.

"But it would be better for your soul," Paul said.

"You mean because you wouldn't be eating at the expense of others?" Jennifer asked.

"Just better, purer," Paul said.

Tim turned on Jennifer. "I really hate to hear people who go to Harvard or Radcliff lamenting their privilege," he said. "Of course we are privileged. Everyone in this room is highly privileged. There has always been privilege, and there will always be privilege. From the privileged classes come the intellectuals and the business leaders. Without them, we'd have chaos."

His cousins stared at Tim, who rarely before had expressed an opinion. Jennifer rose to the bait. "From the intellectuals, the upper middle-class, have always come the social revolutionaries," she said. "Liberating ideas, that's what a university is all about."

But Tim was not going to be led into further argument. "I thought it was all about drinking beer and beating Yale," he quipped. "Want to go out and toss the ball around, Paul?"

The breakfast table was finally cleared and Faith moved into the living room, while Margaret and Anne added a leaf to the dining table. She was beginning to feel a little queasy again, and decided to take another pill.

Frank had warned her against mixing the medication with liquor, so when David served cocktail sherry she asked for juice. Ellen, who had come in from the kitchen, beamed at her.

"I was sure that Paul's grandmother wouldn't drink alcohol," she whispered.

"Not a whole lot," Faith said.

"We are reading George Fox's *Journal* aloud to each other," Ellen continued. "And wow! he was an enlightened one too! Paul said he never heard a word about him at Sunday school."

"First Day School," Faith automatically corrected. "Fox is a little difficult to present to small children. I'm not always sure I understand him myself."

"Our guru says he is one of the chosen ones to bring soul force into the world," Ellen explained patiently.

Faith thought about Joseph and Martha White, and their overland voyage. Perhaps each of her grandchildren, in their own way, was seeking for the sort of faith that had sustained their ancestors, but had been mislaid along the way. Was the search harder today than in her young times? She thought so. We had more help, she mused. Models, ties with the past, a set of values to live by. We had all that, but we didn't always manage to live by it ourselves or to pass it on to our children. We thought they must be free to find out what to believe themselves. But they didn't find much, and they live on borrowed values. Maybe my parent's generation was the last to be really certain, she thought. Or perhaps it went further back. If she kept reading through the papers of those ancestors of hers, would she strike gold for her grand-children?

Her thoughts were interrupted by the roar of a motor-cycle in the driveway. Faith saw Anne stiffen and look at Bert. He glanced at his watch and frowned. Anne shook her head at him. In a few minutes Charlie came in the front hall with Paul and Tim following him. Faith saw that Charlie had trimmed his beard neatly and put on a clean shirt. He kissed his mother, shook hands with his father, then came over to greet Faith warmly. Tension crackled through the room. Jennifer jumped up and went over to her mother, her shoulders hunched in an old ges-ture of concern. Barbara looked stricken.

"Now we need a few volunteers to bring up chairs from the cellar," Margaret said, bustling in, unaware of the electric atmosphere. "O hi, Charlie, we were beginning to be afraid you weren't going to make it."

"I'm here, Aunt Margaret," Charlie said. "What chairs?"

Tim and Paul rose to join him. Faith saw that the three of them were of a height, but standing together their clothes witnessed to the different paths they had taken. Tim, impeccable in gray flannel slacks, a tweed jacket and loafers. Paul wore an Indian cotton shirt, and had let his long hair flow this morning; Charlie with his dark beard and dungarees looked like everyone's notion of an anar-chist. Whatever had happened to produce this diversity? And yet they were alike, three gentle Quaker boys.

"How are you feeling now?" It was Roger, coming to kneel beside her. "I thought you looked a little peaked a while ago."

"It comes and goes," Faith said. "Of course I feel rotten for a few days after the chemotherapy. But it's a very mild dose; I haven't even lost my hair."

"You're thinner, " Roger said. "Eating well?"

"Like a horse. Harriet, the woman I live with, loves to cook," Faith said. "It's surprising, really, how well I do feel most of the time. I suppose something is happening to my insides but Frank, my doctor, doesn't volunteer any information and I don't inquire. I don't see the point."

"New discoveries are coming to light every day," Roger said. "I do believe by the end of the century we may have this thing licked."

"Well, I've had my three score years and ten, and then some," Faith said. "I'd hate to face living on forever and being a confused old lady and a burden on my children."

But later, sitting at the damask clothed table, looking about at her beautiful grandchildren, Faith was seized with such a blinding sense of impending loss that she had to put her fork down for a moment and close her eyes. Not to be at this table next year, not see how all these life stories came out, not to be present for them if they needed her . . . the ache of unshed tears scalded the back of her throat.

She had known this pain before she realized as it began to ebb and she could breath again. Long, long ago, on a rainy June night in England, when she had said goodbye to Alex. The pain of never. She had lived with it for years until it drained away, and she was free to love again.

And then had come the bitter discovery that she had almost lost Tom, during those wasted years when their marriage had been absent minded. And again the pain had come, when Tom died.

"I've had a lot of practice," she reminded herself. "I ought to be good at giving up." But when she looked up, the flames of the tall Thanksgiving tapers swam before her eyes.

Chapter 7

DECEMBER 5, 1968

arly in December it snowed, a thick, wet snow which clung to every twig and branch. Faith and Harriet watched, entranced, as the huge flakes drifted down, swiftly transforming their familiar view of the river into a world of grays and whites. Snow clung to the leaning cedar trees and coated each needle of the jack pine across the river, snow mounded on blueberry bushes and lay like a quilt along the water's edge. Occasionally a chickadee would dart from nowhere to peck at the grain in their feeder. Otherwise all was gentle silence and the soft, drifting snow.

"I think I ought to try it in Japanese brush strokes," Harriet said pensively.

"Of course thee must," Faith told her. "All whites and grays except for the black cap of the chickadee."

She was worried about Harriet. Usually her friend went to Florida each winter to paint and to stay with cousins on the beach. It was a custom that accounted for the nut brown shade of her skin, so startling against that straight white hair. This year however she was refusing to consider such a trip. She had agreed to stay with Faith, she had always wanted to see what it was like to spend a winter on Swallow Creek, and that was that. But she was sometimes silent, and Faith suspected that she was missing the sunshine and her art classes at Sarasota.

"Please do try to paint it," she urged Harriet again. "If it turns out to please thee I'll buy it for a Christmas present for Anne."

Harriet, needing no further urging, got out her paint brushes and established herself at the window. Faith, seizing the opportunity, fetched the White papers. She had been working to get them in chronological order, and she had discovered a twenty page fragment from the journal of a Patience White, who had traveled in the ministry in 1777, quite impervious to the war. With a fellow Quaker minister she had visited Red Bank, New Jersey, where a battle was in progress, and gone on to Trenton, where the British held the town, and the Americans were on barges on the river.

I wrote my dear husband that though we might not meet again, yet I felt sure I had parted from him and our children for the sake of our dear Master. And I prayed he would be found steadfast if the soldiers came to our farm, looking for provisions.

"Can thee imagine it?" she asked Harriet, "Going off and leaving thy husband and children possibly never to see them again? This woman traveled for eighteen months, and as far as I can make out, a child of hers died while she was away. How could she stand it?"

"I don't know," Harriet said. She was frowning, trying to get her charcoals mixed properly. "I guess they had more children in those days, and were more used to their dying."

"I don't think that was it so much," Faith mused. "She says the death of this child was a great trial to her, and that thoughts of home haunted her. But when she was in despair, the Holy Spirit came to her as comforter. I don't know, but the ecstatic way those early Quakers talked about the Spirit, it must have been like falling suddenly and violently in love."

Harriet looked at her curiously.

"Thee knows, the sorts of feelings one has that the whole world has changed. It looks and smells different, and one is living on a whole new plane of being," Faith said. "It takes one completely away from the ordinary world and ordinary emotions, like the day-to-day way we love our husband and children."

"Well, but that was when we were very young, not after we were married," Harriet said.

Faith decided not to pursue it further. "I think it was what they meant when they said they had great openings," she said. "Once or twice in my life I've felt I could understand, but mostly I've just muddled along. This woman was willing to give up her life to follow her leading."

Harriet laid down her brush.

"What is thee saying?" she inquired. "Going off to Algeria when thee was seventy years old? Or for that matter, going to France when thee was twenty-three? Thee certainly ignored the war then? It was just as dangerous and just as sacrificial."

"No, it wasn't really dangerous," Faith said. "And I did it for all sorts of different reasons. To be with Tom, the first time, and to get over his death, the second time. Not because I felt led by the Holy Spirit, exactly."

"I never quite know what thee means when thee speaks of the Holy Spirit," Harriet said tentatively.

"I never quite know either," Faith said. "With my head that is. After I got over the earlier notion of a Heavenly Father like my own earthly one, I've never been able to put down in black and white just what it is that I believe. It's what I feel, not what I think. 'This I knew experimentally,' as George Fox said. But it's been enough to act upon. I think that has to do for most of us in the modern age."

She returned to the journal. Patience White had taken a chill sleeping out under the stars, and thought perhaps she was going to die.

This was a close and trying time for me, so far from my friends and close connections, not knowing but that it might be the Lord's will for me now to depart this life. I labored earnestly to say "thy will be done" but oh, I perceived that it is an awful thing to die so far from ones loved ones. But then it was opened to me that this would not be the case, for the Lord still had work for me to do.

There it was again, that sense of vocation, that absolute purity of purpose. I've lived all my life on the borrowed strength of those convictions, she thought, without ever making them really mine. I've squandered that wealth without producing more. Now I have nothing to pass on to my grandchildren. But give me a little more time, Lord, perhaps I'll find the words.

From the bedroom the telephone jangled. Faith got up carefully and went to answer it. The lilting voice on the other end could only be Elsie's.

"Dearie, I hate to disturb thee, but I thought thee ought to know. It's Florence. She had a stroke last night at dinner, and then passed away very peacefully a few hours later."

"But I just saw her," Faith said, bewildered.

"She was just fine at Thanksgiving," Elsie said. "In fact, she had a good fall. Poor Lowell appears to be taking it well, but one can guess how lost and bewildered he really feels."

"Is the memorial service set?" Faith asked a trifle faintly.

"Yes, tomorrow afternoon at four. But thee mustn't feel thee has to come. I'm sure Lowell and everyone else will understand that thee can't be expected to make it."

"O, we'll come," Faith said. "At least I'll come, and likely Harriet will want to come also."

Faith turned slowly away from the phone. Florence had been her roommate at Wellesley, her bridesmaid, her fellow worker for the AFSC in France, her Haverford neighbor, her friend, her conscience. Gay, bossy, opinionated old Florence. More than anyone else, she had held the past and present together. Faith wasn't always sure she even liked her particularly. She was just there, an element in her life. And now she was gone. It wasn't fair, Faith thought rebelliously. Why can't I prepare to die in peace? Why do I have to go on having my underpinnings knocked out, one by one?

"Of course we'll go," Harriet agreed immediately. Harriet had gone to Bryn Mawr instead of Wellesley and

87

hadn't known Florence quite as well as Faith did. Still, they had been young Friends together before the first world war. Faith and Harriet didn't say much to each other, but they knew what the gathering would be like, a reunion of the thinning ranks of their classmates, along with family and friends.

"If only the roads won't be slippery," Harriet worried.

But the new snow melted that very afternoon, and the next day brought a dispirited winter rain. With Faith at the wheel they drove past rainsoaked cornfields, past a few weathered farm houses and then acres and acres of new ugly boxlike development houses, interspersed with giant supermarkets, used car lots, nightclubs, sex parlors. The trip from Swallow Creek to Philadelphia was becoming a tour of suburban blight. The city itself, gray and dreary in the rain, looked at least more substantial. Just as they came off the bridge, though, Faith had to swerve sharply to avoid hitting an elderly wino on Vine Street. They drove out the Expressway to the Narberth exit, then followed the back road to Ardmore, through woodsy country, pleasant even in the rain.

"One beautiful house after another," Harriet commented.

"Everywhere I go I see privilege," Faith remarked. "I wonder how many Black families live out here?"

"Faith Smedley, thee is beginning to sound like a socialist in thy old age," Harriet said.

"It's my grandchildren," Faith said. "Their influence, and this terrible war that goes on and on."

At the meeting house many cars were already drawn up, and several elderly couples were helping each other over the puddles in the parking lot. Faith saw her sister Jane, draped in a blue plastic waterproof coat, and waved to her. I must invite Jane down to Swallow Creek next weekend, she reminded herself. She's beginning to feel left out again.

Harriet raised a large black umbrella, which looked about as big as she, and together they huddled under it against the driving rain.

Inside, the bare meeting house smelled of wet wool and rubbers. Faith looked around quickly. They were all here, all the old regulars. Her brother Harry and his wife; Allen Morris, retired professor of philosophy; tiny Anne Stone who had taught both her and Florence at Westtown and must be over ninety; the Brinkleys, the Coxes, some younger people from the Service Committee. What veterans of memorial services they all were! Though the family had not yet come in to take their seats, the meeting had already settled into a reverend silence. Faith slipped off her raincoat, settled carefully in the seat, and tried to center down, holding each of her children and grandchildren in the light, as she often did at the beginning of worship.

So Florence was gone. Now that she thought of it, she was ashamed that her first concern had not been for Lowell, the widower, or for Florence herself, who loved life and must have hated to part with it, but for her own precious self. My memories, my underpinnings, she scolded. Me, me, me. It was a new development, the threat of death pushing her to cling more ardently to self and life than ever before. There had been so many good years when she was freed of that concentration on self that was such a plague to the young; years when she had been able to be with people without always wondering how she appeared to them. That freedom had been the secret of making real friends, she discovered. Was it going to crumble away now along with her crumbling health?

There was a slight stir as a line of people came in the front of the meeting. Faith recognized dear, stooped Lowell, his gray hair standing up in jagged peaks, as usual, followed by a middle-aged woman who must be Dorothy, their daughter, then several tall young men and women of the grandchildren generation. A fat, balding man followed. Dear Lord, was that really Peter: and the woman with him must be Mildred. At least Florence's angular cousin from Wilmington, Ohio, hadn't changed beyond recognition. With a soft rustle the mourners sat down on the first bench, and the meeting settled into quiet again.

Was each person in the room remembering the Florence he or she had known? Faith wondered. She suddenly had a ridiculous picture in her mind. Florence in middy and bloomers, her face flushed, her glasses eschew, her hair every which way, arguing hotly with the referee. Yes, she had shot the ball into her own goal, but there'd been interference. This wasp had flown up into her face and buzzed between her eyes till she couldn't see a thing. The memory was so vivid that Faith could smell the rotting pears from the tree midway up the hockey field, see yellow jackets crawling over them, feel her own confusion between amusement and embarrassment for her friend. Florence was so often, so passionately, wrong.

"I remember when dear Florence was my student," a voice quavered from the back of the room. "I was teaching biology at the time, and I remember describing the Lamarckian theory. I thought I had done rather a nice job of it. And then this large girl got up from the back of the room and boomed, 'but how do you know yourself that it isn't true? What's your own experience? What proof have you that it's not?' And you know, I had a hard time answering her. I don't think ever again I was quite so ready to accept something I have received on authority without testing it out in some manner. I've remembered that all my life. To keep on questioning is a rare quality, and Florence had it, and taught it to me, who was supposed to be her teacher."

Faith smiled to herself. Despite the quaver in her voice, Anne Stone sounded exactly as she had almost sixty years ago; brisk, no nonsense, all business. She was in the tradition of the early feminists, believing that a woman's mind was as capable as a man's of hard, abstract, logical thought. Looking always as delicate as a fading bouquet of spring flowers, she was as tough as steel with her students.

There was a shuffling of feet, and some coughing, then a deeper silence settled. Out of long practice, Faith relaxed into it, letting it take her where it would. It was like the river, ever moving, yet ever the same. Sometimes, if you were lucky enough, you were drawn into its current. Not my will but Thine. Was that what Patience White had struggled to experience, fevered and frightened in the wilderness?

"I remember Florence in France as part of our first AFSC contingent," a voice said from the back. Again Faith recognized it without turning. It could only be Jim Balderston. "She was assigned to our *equipe* at Sermaize in the Marne valley. The town was reduced to rubble, but now that the Germans were retreating the refugees were returning. The English Friends got there first and set up a clinic and refugee center, and we joined them primarily to help erect prefabricated houses and to provide transport for the agricultural workers. I might add the British Friends were not always overjoyed by our presence. It was from that experience I learned the meaning of the phrase, 'two people separated by a common language.'"

A titter ran through the meeting house.

"Florence, however, was never one to brook such nonsense. Though assigned to the refugee center, she could drive and sometimes she was called in emergencies to join the transport team.

"I remember one day when all the trucks were out in the field, and an emergency arose at the clinic. One of the patients needed an operation, and had to be driven back to Paris, since his problem was beyond the scope of our frontier methods. There was one old jalopy that we kept at headquarters, and Florence volunteered to try to make the trip with it.

"'But thee can't do it alone' the English Friend in charge objected. 'What if thee has a flat tire? Or a breakdown on a lonely road?'

"'Friend, if thee thinks I don't know how to change a tire thee is very much mistaken,' Florence told him. 'Only a damn fool would drive a car she didn't know how to repair.'

"That was Florence," the voice concluded, as another ripple of mirth died away. "A lovely, vital woman who went at life with the common sense and zest of the early Friends. We are all the richer in spirit for having known her."

Again there was silence, then several people spoke in turn about her contributions to the college community and her work with the local garden club. The statements were pleasant, but the spark and fire of the old Florence did not shine through. Faith wondered if there were something she could add. She almost never spoke in meeting, never feeling quite sure of the Divine nature of the thoughts that rose within her, but a memorial service was a little different.

But now Lowell himself was standing, unfolding his long, awkward body from the cramped bench, turning a bit to face the body of the meeting. "Florence didn't always approve of all I said in meeting," he began wryly. "She thought I had a tendency to wander, which is quite true, I suppose. Still, I think she would want me to speak to her friends today." He paused, and quite unselfconsciously wiped a tear from his cheek.

"Florence knew she might die fairly soon. The doctor had told her after the last attack that it was only a question of time. All summer she was preparing for it, straightening out her papers and making plans for me to carry on, knowing how helpless I'd be. But more than that, she'd been reading and thinking about death, and I think she was quite ready. 'I'm even getting a little excited about dying,' she told me."

He sat down, and the meeting settled into a profound silence. Faith felt goose bumps along her spine. This message sounded as though Florence had designed it for her. She had always directed Lowell in certain things; how to drive, how to salt his food, what socks to wear. Had she directed him to speak today to Faith's condition?

The thing was, she was not making the effort to get ready of which Lowell spoke. She had not yet wrestled with acceptance, not my will but Thine. At the very moment she ought to be detaching herself, she was enmeshing herself more into life; her children, her grandchildren, her Swallow Creek neighbors. Old, bossy, no nonsense Florence was right as usual, and she ought to get busy preparing her mind.

"Lazarus laughed," a woman's voice said near at hand. Faith glanced up, and saw that it was a middle-aged woman who taught literature at Bryn Mawr, and whose name she couldn't quite place. "The title of this play by Eugene O'Neill has always haunted me," the woman continued. "Raised from the dead, restored to life, Lazarus laughed with delight, realizing that he was now free of the fear of death. The need to preserve our identity, to survive, this is the ultimate anxiety, beneath and below all the other fears that hem us in. How beautiful, how joyous life can be beyond those hedges. I think this is the message that Florence's life has for us today. Seize the moment! Seize the hour!"

The woman delivered her last line with drama, in contrast to the quiet understatement of the previous speakers. Nevertheless, the silence of the meeting rose and lapped peacefully over her message. You only die once, Faith thought. But maybe not, maybe every time you give up something precious you have a little experience of dying. And dying, learn to live. Perhaps I don't need to emulate thee, Florence. Perhaps I began my preparations years ago.

Chapter 8

DECEMBER 5, 1968

On the way home to Swallow Creek, the rain turned back to snow. Harriet drove cautiously, and the lights of passing cars flashed by, growing fewer as they approached the dark pine barrens. Soon there was nothing but black sky overhead, and row upon row of spindly pine trees. Faith looked up at the corner of the sky she could see through the car windows, and noticed how the clouds were gathering, and the stars winking out.

"That's funny," she said presently. "The sky is rosy toward the east. The lights at Randall's Corners couldn't be enough to make the sky light up."

"Could it be fire?" Harriet asked. With lips compressed she began to drive a little faster. Faith leaned forward, her throat going dry. It was fire, they could now see the flicker of flames against the clouds. And it was coming from near Swallow Creek.

Passing the Paxton's store, they were overtaken by a fire engine from a nearby town racing along, its siren screaming. It passed the entrance to their cabin, and headed toward the blueberry fields. Harriet followed at a reckless pace, the car bumping in the sand rutted road. They knew before they saw it that it was Angelina's cabin, a mighty burning torch in the surrounding darkness.

A fireman angrily signaled Harriet to pull over. Bemused and frightened, she was about to pull up at the Costas door. Now she wrenched the car over so quickly that it came perilously close to the ditch. The two women sat there for several long moments in shocked silence, trying to take in the scene.

There were two fire fighting companies already present in addition to the one that had just arrived. One group of firemen had stretched a hose to the river and were manning a pump. Something was evidently wrong with the pressure, however, and only a thin stream of water fell on the blazing cabin. Another group had formed a bucket brigade, and a third were chopping energetically at the brush between the cabin and the blueberry fields, trying to create a fire break.

The blaze produced a brilliant light, and a wave of heat. Harriet and Faith could feel it in the car. A number of other cars had driven up, and people stood around watching the fire, mesmerized by the leaping flames. Faith saw that the Stromans were there, looking shocked, then recognized young Donald Platt, wielding an axe, while Susie stood nearby, her baby in her arms.

"Where is Angelina?" Faith asked. "I don't see her. I'm going to look for her."

"Dearie, I'm sure she has been taken care of. Thee ought to sit right here," Harriet said worriedly.

"Harriet Buffum, I am up to here with thy continual fussing," Faith said crossly. She let herself out of the car and found to her fury that her knees were weak. She leaned against the door for a moment to gain strength, then started toward the group of spectators watching the fire. Behind her she heard Harriet's car door bang.

"Better stand back, ma'm. We don't know which way the sparks are going to fly," a man warned.

Faith stepped back obediently, then began to circle the group of watchers. She had not changed into her boots, and her low heeled pumps skidded in the wet sand. Every once in a while the wind drove a cloud of dense smoke toward her, and she coughed and fought for breath. Harriet, now at her side, looked outraged but stumbled along mutely.

As she drew nearer, Faith saw that Susie Platt was holding her baby in one arm, and embracing a woman with the other. It was Angelina, rocking herself back and forth and moaning softly. At her feet lay an old kitchen clock and a couple of saucepans, and a plastic santa claus, evidently things she had grabbed as she left the burning house.

"But where's Juan?" Faith asked, frightened.

Susie pointed to the men chopping the underbrush, and Faith saw the lean figure of Juan, wielding a machete fiercely. He would be afraid of losing his job, she realized.

Faith went up to Angelina, who had her arms clasped about her, and put her hand gently on her shoulder. "I am so sorry," she said.

"We called the electric company, but they wouldn't come," Angelina said. "We called and we called."

"You're freezing," Faith said. "Here, take my shawl." She wrapped the warm wool shawl around the woman's shoulders.

"She ought to go somewhere warm," Susie Platt said. "She's liable to go into shock."

"Why don't we take her back to our cabin?" Faith said. "It's near. She can spend the night. We've got lots of room."

"She may not want to leave with Juan here," Susie said. "Here, you better sit down, Mrs. Smedley. You don't look so good yourself."

There was a rickety wooden chair near by, rescued from the cabin. Faith sank on it gratefully. Her knees were trembling, and pain shot up and down her back. They had stayed for the covered dish supper at the meeting house after the service, and she had forgotten to take her regular pills, she remembered.

The pump was beginning to draw now. The volunteer fire fighters shouted to each other along the length of the hose, then an arc of water squirted from the nozzle, almost knocking down the man who held it, and fell hissing into the middle of the flames. It was too late, though. The cabin was completely enveloped in flames, and the water only served to send a shower of sparks skyward. Some landed here and there in the underbrush, and the firemen scattered to stamp them out.

"I wish Don would be careful," Susie worried. "He's already singed his beard."

Another spurt of water brought another cloud of black smoke and flying sparks. Then, with a volcanic rumble, the little cabin fell in upon itself, sending flames to towering heights. The circle of watchers groaned. Those hungry flames awakened in all of them deep, primitive fears.

Too late, a second hose jerked to frantic life. Between the two streams of water the fire, having nothing to feed upon, was soon subdued. Coals hissed and clouds of dense smoke spread across the entire clearing. Harriet began to choke violently.

"Harriet, thee ought to get out of here," Faith said. "Take Angelina with thee."

"You ought to go too, Mrs. Smedley," Susie said. "I don't like your color."

The firefighters had now trained their hoses on the surrounding brush, where the men had been chopping a fire break. Don Platt detached himself from the group and came up to stand beside Susie.

"I think they've got it under control, now." he said. "And it's starting to rain a little. Susie, you take Angelina to Mrs. Smedley's cabin and I'll bring Juan over later."

A fine, cold mist had begun to fall. Faith shivered, and got slowly to her feet. Her knees were weak again, and her throat dry. For a moment she thought she was going to faint. Instead she took a deep, shaky breath and began to move toward the car, nursing herself along like a child, just one more step, just one more step.

Susie came behind her, leading Angelina, followed by Harriet, still coughing. Faith got behind the wheel, motioning Harriet to sit beside her, while Susie and Angelina climbed into the back. With what felt like the last spurt of her strength, Faith turned the car around and headed back down the rutted lane toward her cabin.

At the door they found the Stromans. "We just wondered if there was anything we could do," Lillian Stroman said. "Is there someone Angelina wants us to notify?"

Susie held up a cautionary hand. Angelina looked gray. "Maybe we ought to give her something for shock," she said hesitantly.

"There's brandy in a bottle below the counter," Faith told her. She stumbled to the nearest chair and sank down, feeling weak. Harriet began to choke again, and Ben Stroman thumped her on her back. Susie deposited her sleeping baby on the couch and helped Lillian find glasses and pour each person a finger of brandy. Lillian gave Angelina a larger helping. Angelina choked on her first swallow, then drank the rest down quickly, her face regaining color.

"I should get word to Stephen," she said.

"Can we call him for you?" the Strohmans asked.

Angelina shook her head. "He doesn't have his own phone," she said. "There's a neighbor who will take messages. But he only understands Spanish."

Faith gestured to her to use the phone. She took a sip of the brandy, then put her glass down hastily. The fire of the liquor knawed hungrily in her stomach. Better not take a chance of awakening an answering fire within.

Angelina however, could not remember the number in Camden to call.

"Does thee think we ought to call David?" Harriet asked, coming over to Faith. She was still red faced, but no longer coughing. "He might hear about the fire and be worried."

Faith took her old friend's hand and squeezed it. "I'm sorry I was so short with thee, dearie. But no, let's not call him tonight. It probably wasn't a big enough fire to make the news. Let's not call until tomorrow."

It was decided to make up beds for the Costas in the small bedroom off the garage, which could be heated quickly with an electric space heater. Angelina objected feebly, but Faith insisted. The Stromans offered to make up the beds. Faith let them, understanding their need to be useful.

The baby awakened, crying, and Susie picked her up and held her to one milk heavy breast. Just then there was the sound of a car outside, and Don Platt came to the door, with Juan Costa beside him. The Puerto Rican looked tired and defeated. Faith wished she could promise him that he would not loose his job but she realized this was probably going to happen.

Angelina seemed to rouse herself at the sight of her husband, and came to his side. They spoke quickly in Spanish.

"Juan says we shouldn't stay here." she translated. "It isn't right."

"Nonsense," Faith said. "Tell him I need some work done on my dock."

That seemed to be the right note. Juan straightened, and accepted a small glass of brandy.

"In our country, Juan was a how you say, a carpenter," Angelina said proudly. "He built a house for the priest."

Having finished his brandy, Juan called a number and spoke to someone in rapid Spanish. Stephen was evidently summoned, for after a hiatus Juan talked for quite a long time, again in Spanish.

At the end of the conversation he sighed deeply. "I must inform the owner," he said.

"Do you have his number?" Faith asked.

"Mr. Paxton, at the store, he has the number," Juan said.

Faith groaned inwardly. This was going to be difficult. Likely the Paxtons knew all about the fire. Perhaps they had been in the crowd. She cringed at the thought of calling them. Couldn't it wait until tomorrow? No, it couldn't.

"We'll say goodnight then," Irene Stroman said. "I'll call in the morning to see if I can help." Faith thanked her for everything, feeling remorseful that she had been so cool to them earlier in the year. Me and my Philadelphia reserve, she chided herself. The Platts left too, with their sleeping child. Harriet, looking gray, went off to bed.

Faith looked at the clock. It was almost twelve. She couldn't call the Paxtons at this hour. Likely the absentee blueberry grower was also sound asleep. "We'll all go to bed and make the calls in the morning," she decided.

Juan squared his shoulders, which had been drooping with fatigue. Men in his country were not to be ordered about by *abuelas*. "Stephen, he thought I better call tonight." he said.

"The police will likely have notified the owner," Faith said. "He might be in a better mood in the morning. Do you know what started the fire?"

"The electric, it kept sizzling and popping where it came into the house," Angelina said. "Juan was afraid to fix it. Where we come from, no electric. We called Mr. Paxton to send the electric many, many times, but they never came."

"It was the owner's responsibility to keep your cabin in good condition," Faith said, with more assurance than she felt. "He cannot blame you for the fire. It was his fault."

Juan Costa looked at her. *You old woman who does not know how the world works* his eyes said.

"I'm going to go to bed now," Faith said. "I'll be glad to call him in the morning and explain."

The Costas retreated to their bedroom in the garage, and Faith opened the front door for a moment to breathe the night air before retiring to her bedroom. It was raining hard now, and the air was raw and full of the acrid smell of the recent fire. She breathed deeply for a moment, then shut the door and made her way to bed.

Despite her exhaustion, she was slow to doze off. Against her closed eyelids the flames danced and spat out sparks, and just beyond the firelight something dark, something evil, something barely understood, seemed to menace her.

In the morning, she awoke late and headachey. Harriet was up and had made breakfast, and reported that the Costas had just left to drive down the lane toward their former home.

"Did they have any breakfast?" Faith asked.

"No, they wouldn't eat," Harriet said.

Faith went to the door and saw the Costas climbing into their battered Chevrolet. She called "Angelina!"

The woman turned obediently, but Juan got behind the wheel.

"Come back and have some coffee!" Faith urged, at the top of her voice. Angelina turned, waved and then continued on her way.

"This is going to be difficult," Faith told Harriet. "How I wish I had gone ahead and put a pullman kitchen in that room next to the garage. David suggested it, so people could visit and still be independent. But I thought it was too extravagant for just one year." She paused. She did not like to remind Harriet that they were racing against time.

Later in the morning the Costas returned, with some blackened household items which they left at a considerable remove from the house.

"You need me to do some work?" Juan asked when Faith came to the door. Faith thought quickly. "Yes, the dock needs repair. There are some loose boards. And I also need a shed built for my wood," she said. "Part of it for wood and part a place next to it to keep garden tools and the like. Right over there near the woodpile."

"You got some lumber?"

"Tell me what you need and I'll order it delivered from the lumber place at Mt. Ephraim," Faith said. She paused. "Did you talk to the owner?"

Juan made a grimace. "He said the fire was my fault. He fired me. He says I have to pay him back for the cabin."

"That's ridiculous," Faith said. "It was his fault. What is his name?"

"Mr. Randall. He lives in Moorestown."

Faith stared at Juan. She had gone to school with John Randall. And his father had been one of the founders of the Swallow Creek community It wasn't possible that a friend of hers, from a good Quaker family, could be the callous owner.

"I'll call him," she told Juan. "But meanwhile you and Angelina are welcome to stay here and I have lots of jobs that need doing. Come in now and have some coffee."

Juan glanced at Angelina, who had been standing nearby. She nodded, and together they entered the cabin by the kitchen door. Juan took a seat at the table, while Angelina fetched mugs for coffee. Faith found some sweet rolls in the freezer and placed them in the oven to heat. While she did this there was a heavy, uncomfortable silence. Murmuring that she would leave them now, Faith retreated to the living room, and called David.

"My God, mother," was all he could say at first.

"Do you know anything about John Randall of Moorestown?" Faith asked. "He evidently owns the blueberry plant."

"He's at the bank," David said. "He's very much an absentee owner. Employs a local farmer to manage the farm in the summer."

"David, the conditions in which they ask their workers to live are appalling," Faith said. "How can it be that we lived right next to the fields and never paid the slightest attention?'

David laughed. "I guess most families went to Swallow Creek to get away, not to get involved," he said.

"And it's probably no worse, possibly better, than most migrant labor camps."

"That isn't good enough," Faith said. "Angelina tells me that when their great nieces come to visit they aren't allowed to swim in the river. And the swimming place next to the bridge is part of our property! Anyway, I want to speak to John Randall. The fire wasn't Juan's fault. And he has been discharged."

"Mother, you've worn yourself out working to change things." David said. "Algeria. South Philadelphia. And now you are supposed to be resting."

"But I can't rest if I have something like this on my conscience," Faith explained.

"You are just too good," David said.

"No, not good," Faith corrected sharply. "Only trying occasionally to do what is right."

But after she had hung up she wondered if she did indeed have the energy to go to Moorestown to meet with John Randall. Perhaps she ought to have asked David to do it for her. She was suddenly completely drained, and decided to lie down for a short nap.

She usually was able to cat nap, waking up refreshed after fifteen minutes of sleep, but this afternoon she slept heavily and awoke, groggy and disoriented in the late afternoon. Harriet was bending over her, looking worried.

"I thought thee would never wake up," she said. "Thee didn't have any lunch, and now it's after four."

Faith struggled to sit up. She was aware that there was something unpleasant she had to do, but she could not remember what.

"Where is Angelina?" she asked.

"The Costas nephew found them a place to stay in Camden and they took off." Harriet told her. "Juan has made out a lumber order for you to place."

Faith got up heavily, went into the bathroom to wash her face and comb her hair. She looked a sight, she thought, haggard and wrinkled.

She had missed her noon pills, and the pain was back. She drank a glass of juice and ate some crackers to get them down. Then she called the lumber company, reaching them just before they closed. They promised delivery tomorrow.

"I don't know why they didn't stay here," Faith said. "It's going to be hard to commute back and forth to Camden in that rattletrap car. They could have stayed at least until we got things squared away with the owner."

"They were uncomfortable," Harriet said. "They'll be able to relax with their own kind."

"Barriers, barriers," Faith complained. "I sometimes think it was easier in Algeria with Mbarka. We didn't have all those years of wall building to undo."

She had to admit, though, that the peace and quiet of her cabin was heavenly. She sat by the window and watched the light fade until the river was only a darker shadow against the further shore. Harriet cooked their simple supper, and brought Faith a glass of wine, which she accepted gratefully.

"I ought to call John Randall," she said, "but not tonight."

"I wish thee wouldn't try to see him at all," Harriet said. "It's only going to upset thee, I'm afraid."

"Being upset isn't always bad," Faith said. "It helps one grow."

She turned back to the fading view, sighing. This precious time, this year of grace, which she had planned to hoard so carefully was being spent profligately on new concerns. She could not have many months left, but now fresh struggle, rather than serenity, lay ahead. What was driving her on like this? As a matter of fact, what had driven her so far? Was she, like her ancestors, somehow caught up in a search for the Light?"

"Maybe before I die I'll come to know what they meant by Light," she told herself.

Chapter 9

DECEMBER 6, 1968

he next morning, before she lost her nerve, Faith called John Randall at his office in Moorestown. He was no longer active in the Society of Friends, and the family had sold their cabin on the river. She hadn't seen him for years, except at occasional school reunions. Nevertheless, his voice lit up when she told him who she was, and he urged her to come to the house, to come to dinner, with him and Enid, that very evening.

"No, John, this isn't a social call. It's about business," she said.

"Now what business could you have with me that couldn't be shared with Enid?" he asked teasingly. "She knows all my secrets. Well, almost all of them."

"It's about the fire at the blueberry plant at Swallow Creek," Faith said.

"O that," John said. "Well, that's all taken care of. We've had the insurance people in. We're fully insured against fire."

"Even if it was caused by faulty wiring that had been reported to you?" Faith asked.

There was a pause at the other end of the line. "Who has been talking to you?" John asked. His voice was considerably less warm and friendly.

"I think you had better let me come in and talk with you," Faith said.

"When did you have in mind?"

"How about this morning, while it is fresh in our minds."

"Impossible," John said. "My dear lady, if you had any idea of how many obligations a person on my position has these days. And all those government forms to fill out."

"I won't take long. I'll be there about eleven," Faith said firmly.

But after she hung up she found she was weak at the knees. My traitor body, she fumed. Harriet saw her face and immediately offered to go with her. "I won't be much good, but at least I can drive," she said humbly.

The December day was raw and overcast, the sky slate gray behind the bare trees, the river frosted with crystals again. The radio had cautioned that snow might begin in early afternoon. Juan was busy building the shed Faith had asked for, sawing the wood on two saw horses he had found in the garage. Angelina, who had been coming every day with Juan, was washing the kitchen floor for the second time that week. It was not always easy having the Costas around, but Faith saw genuine warmth and appreciation behind their shyness, and felt she could come to know Angelina better.

Harriet drove carefully, and they reached Moorestown a little before eleven, and found parking behind the bank.

They were greeted inside by a tall blonde young woman in a very short skirt who said she was John Randall's assistant, and could she get a cup of tea for them? John would be just a minute. She showed them to a comfortable sofa and placed a tray containing a tea pot, cups, sugar, cream, lemon and crackers before them.

"All the comforts of home," Faith remarked rather grimly. She sipped her tea gratefully, and wondered what she was going to say to John Randall. "Let me be guided," she found herself praying.

The girl was soon back, and ushered them into a rather grand office. John was evidently the president of the bank. He came forward to greet them, a tall, strong looking man in his middle seventies, tanned from being out in the sun.

"Faith, you'll never lose your beauty," he said admiringly after he had greeted them both and seated them across the desk from him. "Now what is this about the fire?"

Faith explained that she employed Angelina Costa, and had learned from her about the faulty wiring coming into the cabin. "They reported this time after time to Mr. Paxton and asked him to notify the electric company, but no one ever came," she said.

"Did Costa talk about the wiring to anyone besides you?" John Randall asked, his eyes narrowing.

"Oh yes, I'm sure. To his nephew in Camden, I know."

Randall visibly relaxed.

"You've always been a smart woman, Faith, but maybe at times a bit too trustful," he said genially. "Of course Costa would try to throw the blame on the company. But we never received any report of faulty wiring. No, it was his carelessness that caused the fire. You don't know what these people are like, Faith. Well, I cannot blame them. They are peasants, really, straight from the hills. Many of them have never had electricity before in their life. They lived in mud cabins and cooked over fires. Believe me, I know the conditions. And when we set them up in a camp they don't know how to behave. They don't use the outhouse, half the time, but go in the bushes. And they keep cooking out doors, just like they did in their home villages. And then on Saturday nights they drink their hooch, and the police are busy hauling men away to the emergency wards. Women too, sometimes. I know we shouldn't be prejudiced. But believe me, after all the years in the business, I know these people."

"It is hard for people to know each other when the power is all on one side," Faith said. "I happen to believe what the Costas tell me. I believe it to be the truth."

"We were just getting ready to let Costa go anyway," John Randall continued smoothly. "We gave him the job of watchman as a kindness, but we don't need him. We have an alarm system now and the police check down there regularly."

"But he needs to work," Faith said. "He can't have any savings. And I don't suppose he has unemployment compensation?

"No, we pay by the hour," Randall said. "Can't have the government messing around all the time."

"I wish you would take him back and rebuild his cabin," Faith said. "Surely the insurance will cover that?"

Randall looked at her measuringly. "Let's leave the insurance out of this," he said.

"But if it is shown that the fire is your fault you won't be able to collect," Faith pointed out.

"Faith White Smedley, are you threatening me?" Randall's tone was teasing but his face was cold.

"No, just trying to speak the truth to thee, Friend Randall," Faith said. "Just trying to see what light can be shed on these troubles."

"Well, I'm afraid I'm a backsliding Quaker," Randall said. "A lot of that stuff we learned at Westtown is no good in the real world."

"I find some of it very good," Faith said. "And I live in the real world too." She paused. "I think the American Friends Service Committee has a migrant labor program. It may be that they can help me help the Costas."

"Used to be a fine organization, but it has been taken over by a bunch of radicals." Randall said. "What you ask of me, Faith, is impossible. Even if I thought it was a good idea, which I don't, I'd have to talk my partner into it. And then the blueberry growers association would be on my case. We barely make a profit on that operation. To tell you the truth, I go on with it out of family loyalty. My father cared about it. Can you imagine what would happen to Swallow Creek if I sold out to New Jersey Berries?

"All right, John, I tried." Faith got to her feet. "Come Harriet, we'd better get on the road before the snow begins."

A few wet drops brushed the windshield as they started, and by the time they reached Swallow Creek, large flakes were drifting down, as though shaken from a giant pillowcase. Faith watched them with the same surge of joy she had felt as a child at the promise of snow. By the time they had had their lunch it was snowing in earnest. It was hard to see across the creek as the wind drove the snow into dancing sheets.

"The radio says we might get six inches," Harriet ventured, coming in from the kitchen. She added in a whisper, "she's washing the dishes."

"I think the Costas better start for Camden," Faith decided.

"If only the electricity doesn't go off," Harriet worried.

"Even if it does we have kerosene lamps and lots of firewood," Faith pointed out. "Dry fire wood, thanks to Juan."

The Costas were reluctant to leave the two old women by themselves, but Faith insisted. Juan had not asked, and she had not said anything about her interview with John Randall. She wanted to wait and think about what she was going to do next.

After they left she got out a large box of family papers and settled herself by the window, where she could glance up from time to time to watch the dancing curtain of snow. It was so dark she found she had to turn on the light over her shoulder to make out the fading handwriting of the journal she was trying to read.

This woman, Lydia White Morris, was born in 1748 and died in 1818. She was a Quaker minister, much given to travels up and down the American colonies. She waited upon the Lord for guidance in the smallest detail; where to go next on her journey, which ship to take, which traveler on the road to speak to, much as a traveling salesman might wait for word from the head office. Several times she visited a frontier meeting, and sat waiting in vain for the Lord to speak through her, though families had come from miles around to hear the famous Quaker preacher.

Faith thought she was an admirable woman, but found portions of the journal dreary going. Lydia Morris sounded sanctimonious to her, and her meditations sometimes lugubrious. Faith found she skimmed the portions where she wrote about her intense inward sufferings, trying to subdue her will to the Lord's. She couldn't help wondering if Lydia really believed herself to be as inadequate as she professed. Could one distrust oneself so thoroughly and yet still think of oneself as a child of God? It seemed to her the earlier Whites had more joy about them.

And yet . . . and yet. She read for a second time a letter describing Lydia's visit to a Quaker community in upstate New York. Having spoken to her satisfaction at the quarterly meeting held at that place, she was preparing to leave with her companion for religious service on Long Island, when she felt an inexplicable stop in her mind. *My mind was thoughtfully engaged to know to what end I was thus commanded to linger, with all prospect of religious service removed,* she wrote. *I was sunk under such a weight of exercise that I thought I would lie on my bed.* At this moment a Friend came to see her with the terrible news that three young children of the meeting had ventured out on the ice of a nearby pond, and had fallen through and drowned. Lydia went immediately to sit with the families of the bereaved, and to prepare for a meeting for burial. Here she felt filled with the Holy Spirit. *I had a laborious time amongst them, but trust, through Divine help, the free and everlasting gospel was preached and truth not dishonored.*

Coincidence? It seemed unlikely. Rather it appeared to Faith that Lydia had been led, or nudged, by a premonition beyond her five senses. Perhaps I have occasionally been nudged too, Faith thought, though I don't call it by that name.

Chapter 10

DECEMBER 24, 1968

She had given way at Thanksgiving, but for Christmas Faith decided to be adamant. She was going to have the family join her for supper Christmas eve at Swallow Creek.

"Everybody can bring things," she told Margaret. "Thee can roast a turkey if thee likes and bring it along, and we'll just eat on paper plates in front of the fire. It will be simple and beautiful, thee'll see."

Reluctantly, and with many misgivings, the family agreed. Faith was unquestionably a little thinner, except for her distorted stomach, and a little paler than she had been at Thanksgiving, a month ago. On the other hand, it seemed clear that she was holding her own beyond their fondest hopes, and that her spirit was a force to be reckoned with. Consulted, Frank Stoddard said that in his opinion Faith was the best judge of her own capacities, and ought to be allowed free rein.

"The Pine Barrens were made for Christmas." Faith told Harriet happily, coming in one morning with an armful of sand laurel. Already heaps of cedar and ground pine and bayberry were strewn the length of the table. "I don't know whether to bring it all indoors or leave it outdoors, so we can enjoy the view."

"Some of both," Harriet suggested. "Thee'll want to decorate the hearth and the table, and maybe we can get Juan to put some long leaf pine boughs up on the rafters. It is going to be so lovely that I wish I were staying to see it."

Harriet's children had gotten together and bought her a ticket for Florida for two weeks. Faith had been able to persuade her to go by arguing that she needed the room to house Anne and Roger and their four children, counting the new bride. Happy though she and Harriet had been together, Faith thought it was time they had a break from one another. Harriet was at times too brightly cheerful, too terrified of facing painful realities, too protective. Faith found herself sometimes annoyed with her old friend, and this used up precious energy.

Anyway, she was glad to contemplate having at least some of the children under her roof Christmas eve. Lucy and Bert would stay with David and Margaret, and they would all return to Swallow Creek Christmas morning to open the presents.

The thought of the bustle made Faith a little apprehensive. She had grown used in the past months to the peace and solitude of the river, to letting a thought bubble up in her mind and hang there while she explored its many facets. She liked to talk to people one at a time now, more she found unsettling. Still, it was only once, and it was family.

"Thee'll have a lovely time in Sarasota, and when thee comes back we can be hermits together," Faith told Harriet. "I could just stay here week after week, not seeing anyone or doing anything, just contemplating this."

She indicated the window in a sweeping gesture. The view was improving as the season progressed, they thought. A sprinkling of old snow and frost coated the forest floor, turning the fallen leaves into a bed of iced cornflakes. Against the whiteness, the greens and reds were brilliant. It was very cold today, and the river poured through its banks like a sheet of molten green glass. At the water's edge, a lacy frill of ice crystals had formed, and every twig touching the surface of the water wore a pear shaped droplet of ice which glittered in the light.

"If thee'll find the candlesticks I'll show thee how to make little wreaths for them of sand myrtle," Harriet volunteered. "We used to come down here to get it for decorating the meeting house for Christmas supper."

"Shouldn't thee be packing?" Faith asked. Harriet was supposed to leave late that afternoon in order to spend the night in Philadelphia before taking an early plane for Florida.

"I'm all packed," Harriet said brightly. "Anyway, Faith, I do wish thee would come up to Philadelphia with me. I don't like to think of thee all alone here."

"For only one night?" Faith asked. "What could possibly happen to me? We haven't exactly been harassed by intruders down here."

"Yes, but it bothers me," Harriet said. She hesitated, then confessed in a burst. "I spoke to Angelina and she is going to stay until evening."

"O Harriet you didn't!" Faith exclaimed. "She'll be busy with her own Christmas preparations. And I've asked you time and again not to fuss so! It upsets me."

Harriet looked stricken. But she knows I don't like it, Faith thought. Why can't she respect my wishes? "Well, it's done," she said. "Let's forget it. I'll fetch the candlesticks."

By afternoon, the cabin was fragrant with pine greens, and Harriet had made a final batch of Christmas cookies as her contribution to the coming festivities. Feeling remorseful for her earlier burst of anger, Faith gave her her Christmas present early. It was a folding easel, which Harriet could set up on the beach. Harriet's package for her was small and squishy—Faith suspected knitted foot huggers.

Around four, when the sun was already beginning to set, Harriet's son and daughter-in-law arrived for her, and with many admonitions to Faith, Harriet finally got into the car and was driven down the long lane. Faith drew a long, shaky breath of relief when at last they were out of sight. She needed to be away from Harriet's chatter, she realized. Angelina had finished her cleaning and had retired to the bedroom off the garage. In some place deep inside her, deeper than thought, something was arranging itself, sorting itself out, preparing for what lay ahead. It was as though she were involved, day and night, in an inward process to which she needed to give more of her attention.

She sat for a long time by the window, watching the last light fade and the sky grow slowly navy blue as the first stars pricked their way out, one by one. When it was quite dark she sighed, turned on the light, and went to the trunk where she kept the White papers. It seemed like a good night to commune with those long dead ancestors of her.

A packet of letters written in a clear, spidery hand caught her eyes. Her father had attached a label, *1851–1868, Letters of Abigail White Whitson, Philadelphia.* Faith undid the bindings and unfolded the first letter, careful to avoid breaking the brittle paper.

At first glance the letter seemed impossible to decipher. Though the writing was clear it was cramped, and the ink faded. At the bottom of the page the writer had turned the sheet and written across the preceding lines, evidently in an effort to save paper. Gradually, with the help of magnifying glasses Faith was able to make some of it out. The writer was anticipating a meeting planned for fifth day next, a meeting at which the location of the colored school on Catherine Street would be settled. She hoped that Sarah Mapps Douglass, that shining example of her race, would consent to be present, and to teach the Bible course for the mothers. Perhaps Sarah Douglass could also teach physiology, having recently completed a course at the Female Medical College. That such a woman was still asked to sit on the back bench at Arch Street was more than Abigail could bear.

Fascinated, Faith read one letter after another. Abigail was the daughter of a wealthy Friend, and had been raised in the bosom of conservative Quakerism. But she was clearly, a rebel. She corresponded with Ann Preston, founder of the Woman's Hospital, who had assembled a

Board of lady managers to oversee this institution, rather than the usual board of wealthy and well connected men. Through Sarah Douglass, she was in touch with the Philadelphia Female Anti-Slavery Society, an interracial, interdenominational group, whose radical actions regularly appalled more conservative Friends. She seemed to have supported many of their actions, and through them undertaken to educate a young woman escaped from slavery.

Though her writing was stiff and prosy, Faith detected a fiery spirit in Abigail. Why hadn't she heard more about this ancestor? Was it possible that genes from her had stirred her own adventurous life, and were now at work in the more radical of her grandchildren? She went through the letters a second time, trying to choose one to read to the family over Christmas dinner. But the spirit she wanted to expose them to came in snippets, here and there, rather than in a single letter. After a while she got out a pad of paper, and began copying a phrase here, a phrase there.

A knock on the cabin door interrupted her. When she opened it a short young man with curly dark hair stood on the entrance. For a moment she was startled and apprehensive.

"I'm Stephen Costa," the young man said hastily, sensing her fear. "My aunt, that's Angelina, works some for you. I've come to fetch her."

"O Stephen, forgive me, come in," Faith said.

The young man stepped into the room, carefully wiping his feet on the mat. "You were very kind to take my uncle and aunt in after the fire," he said. "We appreciate that."

"It was nothing," Faith said. "I'm only sorry your uncle lost his job. I wish I could do something about that."

Stephen shook his head slowly. "Well that is the way things go," he said, and Faith heard all the years of struggle and disappointment in his voice.

"They need not go that way," she said fiercely.

"Would you like me to build up your fire?" Stephen asked.

Faith was on the verge of saying no, but she suddenly thought it might be more courteous to allow him to do some little thing.

"Why yes, that would be very nice," she said.

Stephen Costa went out to the woodpile and returned, bringing with him the scent of cold, piney air. Businesslike, he went to work laying fresh kindling and logs on her dying coals. Afterwards, when the fire flamed up nicely, she gave him a cup of cocoa.

"Will you celebrate Christmas with your aunt and uncle?" she asked.

"Yes, and my wife and children," Stephen said. "The youngest was born in September."

"O dear," Faith said. "I thought you were much younger than that." She paused, mortified. He was young, as young as her grandsons, she realized. But in his culture, people married early. "What is the name of your baby?" she asked.

"Alexandre," Stephen said. He pulled out his wallet and showed Faith a picture of the baby, then another of his wife and three older children, two girls and a boy. The girls were larger than Faith expected, preadolescent. They wore white dresses, and had their hair in braids. They looked scrubbed, immaculate. And these were the children who were not allowed to swim in Swallow Creek!

Faith complimented Stephen on his family, and found a box of nuts to give him to take back to them. Stephen went for Angelina, and the two wished her a *Felice Novidad* with shining eyes.

When they had left, Faith poured herself a small glass of sherry and turned off the lights. Outside, the stars sparkled frostily against the blackness, and within the fire roared and gave off sparks. She would get up soon and fix herself what little supper her sensitive stomach could bare, but it was nice just to sit here, enjoying every moment of the pure silence.

The next morning she awakened to snow, fine, dry, insistent. A curtain of snow danced across the river and half obscured the opposite bank. When she looked out back she could not see the garage through the blinding sheets of snow that whirled between it and the house. The jack pines were already bent under a heavy burden of snow, and the road was piled high.

Around noon, just as she was beginning to get a little alarmed that the blizzard would last all day, the snow began to slacken. Shortly after two a yellow snow plow appeared, pushing its way down the drive toward her house. When it came nearer she opened the back door and got a glimpse of Mr. Paxton, wearing a red checked wool cap with ear muffs, sitting at the wheel and looking determinedly ahead.

"Come in and have some coffee," she shouted through cupped hands. But he seemed not to hear, and with a final shove of neatly curled snow, backed out of the drive.

Faith remembered that the Swallow Creek Association paid him something each year to keep the roads open in winter. She had assumed that he would hire help for that job. He looked too old and thin and frail for the task. And he had looked angry, she thought. After the confrontation with him she had done all her shopping at Mt. Ephraim. He must feel bitter, having to plow me out.

By five, the snow had dwindled to a few idle flakes and the stars were beginning to come out. She laid a fire, moving painfully between woodbox and fireplace, and was glad when it flared up. It was growing colder, and she was content to sit close to the flames, and be still.

Suddenly, headlights raked the darkening cabin and there was one, no two cars in the drive. Car doors banged, people shouted and stomped, and then in a burst her peaceful cabin was overwhelmed by the entrance of a race of giants. Her children and grandchildren all seemed larger than life, enhanced with quilted jackets, mufflers, hats, mittens, snow boots.

There was a flurry of greetings and cold kisses. Margaret took up a station by the door and began to direct traffic; the turkey and ham in the oven, the rest of the food onto the kitchen counter, jackets and mufflers into one of the unheated bedrooms. All the Krueger's luggage into Harriet's vacated room.

David, coming to stand by his mother, smiled wryly. "A great traffic manager, my wife," he said, rubbing Faith's hand with his big thumb.

Eventually, a sort of order was restored. Bert Levering directed the boys to fetch more wood for the fire, Anne and Lucy helped Margaret in the kitchen, Jennifer mixed mulled cider and hot buttered rum. Other grandchildren exclaimed over the cottage, darted out into the inky night for forgotten packages, draped themselves on the couch or the cushioned window seats.

"But grandmere, don't we need a tree?" Jennifer asked.

"I thought one of the boys could cut a jack pine tonight," Faith said. "I've spotted a couple of beauties out back, and heaven knows we have pines to spare."

"Women can cut trees as well as men," Jennifer said.

"First though, let's eat," Margaret suggested. "If only to make more room for people to sit down."

At Faith's direction, Jennifer lit the candles, each ringed with its tiny wreath of sand myrtle. When they were all ablaze it was possible to turn off the electricity and still have enough light. Margaret and Lucy lined up the platters and casseroles of food along the kitchen counter and everyone helped himself or herself buffet style, Susie bringing a plate to Faith where she sat by the fire.

"Not nearly that much, dearie, please give it to someone else and let me have some really tiny portions," Faith said. Her stomach was more unsettled than usual by the excitement.

Finally, everyone had a plate and a place to sit.

"Before we start may we have just a moment of Quaker silence?" she asked.

They all bowed heads, and quiet settled over them. Faith had meant to make it very brief, but it widened and deepened within and around her. She felt a tenderness for her beloved family and something more, gratitude. It seemed suddenly as though Tom were standing just behind her, with his hand on her shoulder, enjoying the moment with her. "Old girl, we did it. Despite all our troubles, we did it."

Faith raised her head at last and gave David's hand a special squeeze. Later, while they ate, it was indeed as though Tom were present. The special brand of family joking which he had always initiated prevailed. Even her serious grandchildren seemed to fall into the mood, reminding each other of shared memories both here and in the Poconos. The time Paul put motor oil in the pancake syrup bottle and forgot to tell. The time Jennifer lost the top of her bathing suit water skiing, and didn't know it.

After dinner, Jennifer and Tim went out to cut a tree, while the rest of the family began to sing Christmas carols. Faith lamented that she couldn't join them. The strict Quakerism of her childhood had robbed her of musical skills. By the time the rules were relaxed it was too late for her generation to learn. Anyway, like many members of the White family, she had a poor ear. Could music be bred out by generations of custom? It didn't seem likely.

The young of her family at least seemed to have strong, true voices. "O little town of Bethelem," they sang, and "Bring a Torch, Jeanette, Isabella," and "O Holy Night" in both French and English. Faith sighed deeply with contentment. What more could an old woman want. The deep sense of Tom's presence tonight was frosting on the cake.

When Jennifer and Tim returned with the tree, Faith brought out a large box of well worn and beloved ornaments she had saved over the years. The grandchildren exclaimed over them as they decorated the tree. Afterwards, everyone brought presents to place under it, so many presents and they reached well along the floor in all directions. It was time now for each to wish each Merry Christmas and bid each other goodnight, while the Smedleys and the Leverings headed back to Philadelphia. Exhausted beyond the point of sleep, Faith at last slipped gratefully into her bed. Outside the window, stars twinkled in the frosty sky, and a pine tree laden with snow glittered faintly in the star light.

"O Holy Night," Faith whispered to herself. It would be her last Christmas. She ought to be feeling sorry for herself. Instead she felt exhilarated by the challenges of her family and the tasks before her. "I'm getting a little excited about dying," Florence had said. That was the real miracle, the inner life, the unexpected burst of growth, the constant drama of rebirth.

Chapter 11

JANUARY 21, 1969

The snowy Christmas was followed by a January thaw. Snow melted to a few dirty patches under the trees, the lacy ice crystals disappeared from the river's edge, and even the backwater ponds showed open ripples. Moss along the banks glowed brilliant in the dampness, and the tips of the blueberry bushes were already brighter from rising sap.

Harriet, bronzed and rested from her two weeks in Florida, was finishing up a canvas she had started at Sarasota. The brilliant blues and lavenders and aquamarines looked odd in contrast to the subtle mauves and grays of Swallow Creek.

The gentle, mild days lulled Faith. She was tired, she had to admit, from the holidays. The children, overcoming their initial apprehension, had made too much of her apparent resilience. Margaret had organized a New Year's Day buffet at the Chestnut Hill house for the entire White and Smedley connection, as well as a few of Faith's oldest friends. Faith had enjoyed seeing everyone, but she grew tired of having to deal tactfully with their embarrassment and concern.

"Why is death so embarrassing a subject?" she asked her son-in-law Roger. "I don't want all this false optimism. And I certainly don't want everyone reassuring me that it isn't going to happen. I just want as much naturalness as possible."

Roger himself looked embarrassed. "They're saying that it's the new taboo," he said. "In the nineteenth century sex was hidden, but the death bed scene was big in literature and the theater. Now we've got a reversal."

"The bedroom scene is big and death is never mentioned?" Faith queried, smiling.

"Something like that," Roger said uncomfortably.

"Well, they ought to consult the dying," Faith said. "I don't mind talking about it. In fact, it helps. I'm coming to grips with the thing intellectually. Frank says that as far as he can see the cancer is being held at bay with the small amount of chemotherapy I'm taking. I suppose when it really kicks up again I'll see how brave I really am. But right now it's a strain when everyone acts brightly as though nothing were going to happen."

Her own family seemed determined not to acknowledge what was coming. Only Beth seemed able to deal with it.

"Is thee going to bring thy Rich to see me later this winter?" Faith had asked.

"O grandmere, I'd love to have him know thee and see the river," Beth said. "Perhaps in April if thee is still feeling okay by then."

Now, alone with Harriet day after peaceful day, Faith slowly regained her equilibrium. She worked over the Abigail Whitson White letters, excerpting more passages she wanted to keep, puzzling over illegible parts. There were letters which Abigail had received from Ann Preston, the head of the Woman's Hospital, and later from Caroline Still, the second Black woman to graduate from that hospital. Faith thought they were valuable, and decided that next time she went to Haverford she would drop them off for safekeeping at the library.

In mid January, in the middle of all this healing peace, Sylvia Shipley called to invite Faith to a special dinner celebrating the one hundredth anniversary of the founding of the Spring Street Community Center.

"I'm really not going much of anywhere these days," Faith demurred.

"Yes, but this is special," Sylvia insisted. "I wasn't supposed to tell thee, but the fact is that they want to give thee an award."

"An award?" Faith asked. "I don't deserve an award."

"Thee has the longest service of any board member," Sylvia said. "And thee was chair at a crucial time."

"I went off and deserted them for two years when they were having that capital fund drive," Faith argued.

"Dearie, it is not me, and it is not the board, it's the people of the neighborhood who are insisting," Sylvia said. "I know thee isn't feeling well, but if thee possibly could come, it would mean so much to them."

Harriet bristled with indignation. "Who do they think they are, dragging thee out for their old anniversary?" she demanded. "Sylvia Shipley knows perfectly well thee's been ill and hasn't been going anywhere. Just when thee was beginning to look a little less peaked. If thee cannot bring thyself to say no, I will. I'd like to give them a piece of my mind."

"Don't scold me, Harriet," Faith said. "I have a wonderful idea. Why doesn't thee come with me? Then, when I begin to feel tired we can leave early. I do feel I ought to make the effort. I've been on that board since Anne went to Westtown. And working there was my salvation when I came back from Algeria. It kept me rooted and gave me important things to do."

Harriet continued to grumble, but seeing that Faith had made up her mind, agreed to be her chauffeur and companion. In preparation for the trip, she insisted on afternoon naps and early bedtimes, and watched the weather forecast like a hawk.

The days remained mild and cloudy. On the morning of the anniversary, a fine rain set in, but it grew no colder. The two dressed in warm wool suits, lined raincoats and boots, and set off in late afternoon, waving goodbye to Angelina, who had spent the day cleaning the cabin and was just finishing up.

The Spring Street Community Center was located in a downtown section of Philadelphia which had seen better days. One hundred years ago it had been a well-to-do neighborhood. The Whites had been among the comfortable Philadelphia families to live here, occupying one of the large, high ceilinged, three-story brick houses, complete with marble steps and lintels. Block after block of these sturdy houses were now crumbling into disrepair, chopped up into small apartments, shared by many Black and Puerto Rican families.

The community center itself had been started by wealthy matrons of the area one hundred years ago to provide day care for working mothers in the adjacent milltown where Polish and Irish immigrants lived. The Irish and Polish had left long ago, their places taken by the Italians, who also left, followed by the Jews, followed by other Eastern Europeans, followed by African Americans. Faith had been fascinated to discover that each of these groups had left small pockets behind: an Irish Catholic church, a tiny synagogue, a frightened handful of older men and women who dared to venture out only in broad daylight, clutching their purses and shopping bags tightly.

At the turn of the century, at the height of immigration, the board of the Spring Street Community Center had erected a large building, complete with banquet hall, stage, basketball court and classrooms. For twenty years, all these facilities were in full use, but with the changing times, the activities moved elsewhere, and it hadn't been possible for the board to justify spending the money to keep up all the facilities. With the advent of Black Power, it had been necessary to hire a Black executive, who in turn had hired a largely new Black staff. They had had little success so far, however, in establishing themselves with the neighborhood. Now the Center limped along, half-empty, serving mainly the very young and the very old.

Tonight, however, the banquet hall was to be filled. Long trestle tables had been laid out in a U shape, covered with plastic clothes and decorated with bright plastic flowers.

"I would have loved to have the Robertsons do the flowers, but the neighborhood ladies on the committee wanted to do them themselves," Sylvia Shipley whispered to Faith.

"And quite right too," Faith said. She looked around eagerly and recognized old friends. Jane McBrian, a woman of Irish descent who had taught jewelry making for twenty-five years. Lou Pemberton, the bookkeeper who alone had managed to survive the Black Power upheaval of recent times. Al Bustill, the Black basketball player who had grown up in a center family, and remained loyal to the old ways. Others, whose names she could barely remember, came crowding around her. "We miss you, Miz Smedley." "How you been, Miz Smedley, you lookin' a bit peaked."

"Come, dearie, sit down," Sylvia said, leading her to the head table. "Thee can talk to people without standing up and wearing thyself out. Thee come too, Harriet."

Faith surrendered her raincoat. Looking about she began to wonder if she ought to have dressed more formally for the occasion. Her good tweed suit set her off for what she was, a board member. The women of the neighborhood had donned satins and sequins for the banquet. Some were in full evening gowns. When Sam Gannett, the new Black director, came forward to pin an orchid on her shoulder she thought that she might at least have worn a good black dress in honor of the anniversary.

She had been on the committee that had hired Sam last year, one of her last acts before her operation.

"How are things going?" she asked. "I read the minutes, but I don't seem to absorb the information."

"O, pretty good," Sam said. "The fund didn't make its quota last year so we got cut, and we had to raise some extra money. But things are coming along pretty well. We're going to get an outreach program going for the elderly, and Joe's starting some drill team training."

"Drill teams?" Faith asked. "Back into recreation?"

"Well, it's what the people of the neighborhoods want," Sam said.

Faith smiled. She remembered when the center had been trying to get out of providing recreation, in competition with the city's nearby recreation center, and putting more of its staff work into community development. But now community control was the watchword, and what the community wanted, the community got. Faith wasn't sure the new staff knew the community well enough to know what it did want. It was nice though to no longer feel a sense of burning responsibility about such issues. A little like having one's children grow up. Only the neighborhood people were not her children, and never had been. It had been the mistake of well intentioned board members in time past to think so.

"Do you have Latino youth in the drill teams?" she asked.

Sam hesitated. "Doesn't seem to work to mix the groups," he said. "The Latinos tend to stick to themselves."

"But you have programs for them as well?"

"Well, we've been thinking about starting some carpentry classes for them."

"I've got just the man to teach them," Faith said. "I'll call you."

The tables were now full. She looked around at the familiar faces of the few of the old guard that remained. Sylvia Shipley, Donald Platt, senior; John Newell, her cousin, Bill White. The rest of the faces were dark, and many of them were new to her. When she had resigned, to be replaced by a Black board member, Bill White had argued with her.

"But Faith, surely we don't want an all Black board?" he said. "Friends have always believed in integration, not separatism."

"We've practiced Quaker separatism long enough," Faith reminded him. "Separate schools, separate vacation places, Quaker intermarriage. We of all people ought to understand the urge to create a separate identity."

Bill had looked puzzled, but Faith had not only resigned but helped to recruit a Black lawyer, Dick Wells, for the new chairman of the board. Now Dick tapped his glass, and the group rose, while a local Black minister gave the blessing. He asked the Lord to be with them, to make them thankful for the occasion, and for those who had gone before, including the Reverend Brother Martin Luther King, whose birthday was last week, and whose sacrifice for his people would never be forgotten.

Then the women, wearing plastic aprons over their party dresses, went into the kitchen and returned bearing steaming platters; turkey and ham, canned peas, mashed potatoes. There were dishes of cranberry sauce, of celery and olives, of rolls and butter already on the tables. Someone at one end of the table loaded plates to over-flowing and passed them around.

The usual banquet fare. Faith sighed and picked up her fork, hoping that Dick Wells on her right and Sam Gannett on her left would not notice her lack of appetite. Polite dinner conversation was really not necessary here. Faith attempted to ask Dick about his wife and children, but it was almost impossible to hear his answers against the roar of the crowd, and she soon gave up and lapsed into silence, while she toyed with her food. She was glad when the plates were cleared away and the desert, a chocolate ice cream roll, was served along with bitter coffee.

Now the program for the evening began. A large Black woman dressed in a red satin evening gown sang "America" rather beautifully. Dick Wells introduced new staff members. Sam Gannett made a brief report on recent community activities.

Next, a tall slim Black girl with a large, soft Afro was introduced and began to read a speech from some papers which she held. The speech was evidently not her own, for she stumbled over unaccustomed words and swallowed the ends of her sentences. At first Faith could make little of it. Then she caught the phrase, "one who stood by us in our hour of need," and knew this was a tribute to herself. She strained to listen. "One who understood our need for self-determination." The author must be from the staff or from the neighborhood. Perhaps Sam? She looked at him inquiringly and he smiled back noncommittally. She was touched. A memory of afternoons spent in this neighborhood, trying to help a little Black boy learn to read, or calling on a frightened

Ukranian grandmother, came back. Yes, they had given her far more than she had given them.

The girl finally came to an end, and sat down to applause. Sam rose and came forward to hand Faith a package, and she unwrapped it gingerly. It was a large wooden plaque, in the shape of a shield, with her name and the dates of her service on the board in brass letters.

"I'll cherish this always," she promised them. "And I'll always remember this night and your generosity to me." She looked about the room, seeing their answering joy, and felt a surge of love for them all. If only she could be around a little longer to see how things came out. Always, she thought, had been an odd choice of words.

"Whatever will thee do with that plaque?" Harriet asked when they were at last in the car and heading toward the Ben Franklin bridge. "Rather military for a Quaker, isn't it?"

"Hang it in my bedroom," Faith said. "Look at it whenever I need a lift."

She leaned back, exhausted. There must be no more trips like this. Her life by the river, her ancestors' journals, her preoccupations with her own family, were enough for her meager store of energy.

Chapter 12

January 29, 1969

ate in January, the heaviest snow of the season came. Flakes began drifting down at noon, and by evening they were sheeting down in blinding curtains. The lights dimmed and flickered several times, but continued to burn. Juan Costas built them a roaring fire before he and Angelina left for Camden, and Harriet, seizing control of the kitchen, filled the cabin with the wonderful smell of an old fashioned lamb stew.

Faith, who had been reading an ancestor's journal, took off her glasses, rubbed her eyes and stretched. She felt better than she had at any time since Christmas. Lydia White had written that she believed that the Holy Spirit must be keeping her alive beyond her time for some purpose. She was not worried about the reprieve, as Lydia might have been. It was heavenly.

The next morning she awoke to a dazzle of light. The sun was shining on a transformed world. In the course of the night the snow had changed to a freezing rain, and now every twig and leaf glittered with a thousand diamonds, and the snow was crusted with a gleaming icing.

They were at breakfast when the phone rang. "Is thee all right, mother? Do you have power?" David asked.

"Lots of power," Faith told him gaily. "We were pretty well snowed in, though, and on top of that we had an ice storm. Did you?"

"Nothing is moving here, but the temperature is due to go up," David said. "Better call Mr. Paxton to plow you out."

"I'd rather not," Faith said, sighing. "Can't we find someone else than Paxton?'

"Mother, be practical," David said. "Who else can we get in the middle of digging out from a blizzard. I'll call him if thee like."

"All right, but we have to talk about him," Faith said. "Him and a lot of others down here."

David sighed. "Thee is incorrigible, mother," he said. "But all right, we'll talk. Meanwhile I have a surprise for thee. Lucy is here. She wants to come over and see thee this afternoon. She tried to call thee from Boston yesterday, but I guess thy phone was out for a while."

"Is something the matter?" Faith asked.

"Not that I know of," David said. "She just wants to visit with thee, she says."

"That was David," Faith told Harriet, returning to the breakfast table. "He's coming over this afternoon if he can get through and bringing Lucy with him. She wants to spend the night."

"She can have my bed," Harriet said.

"Nonsense, we'll put her in the guest bedroom," Faith said. "Angelina has it all made up with fresh sheets."

After breakfast Faith called Sam Gannett. The phone rang six times before someone answered. When she asked for Sam, she was told they were all out shoveling snow. She made a note to herself to try again the next day, and returned to her desk, thinking it might be a good time to catch up on letter writing.

The sun was brilliant all morning, and the ice melted quickly. Around noon the big snow plow came up the lane, cutting blue curved shadows into the dazzling white. Faith looked out the back window, but saw that the man in the cabin was not Mr. Paxton. She waved, intending to ask whoever it was in for coffee, but he was intent on his work and did not see her.

David and Lucy arrived shortly after lunch. Lucy was dressed jauntily in a bright pink ski jacket and black pants with a pink stripe, but she looked thin and anxious, Faith thought. She gave them both a cup of tea and cookies, and sat at the kitchen table with them while they ate.

"How did thee make out with John Randall?" David asked.

"Not well," Faith said. "He won't take Juan back, or rebuild their cabin. I thought about getting in touch with the insurance company, and telling them about the defective wiring, but I'm not sure we could prove the Costas' story in a court of law."

"Does Juan want to go back?" David asked.

"He needs a way to earn a living," Faith told him. "Actually, I am seeing if Sam Gannett can use him to teach carpentry. He's a skilled carpenter, and the center has a new Puerto Rican populaton."

"Won't that solve the problem?"

"That would be only part time. I'm also going to try to find work for him in Mt. Ephraim. Syliva can help. But David, they need a place to live, and I think they like it here. I've got an idea about that."

David looked wary. "Not sure I like the sound of that."

"We'll talk about it another time," Faith said.

After David left, Faith suggested that they take a little walk. "I've been cooped up here so long I'm getting cabin fever."

"Is thee sure thee's up to it, mother?" Lucy asked.

"I'm feeling fine, actually better than I did a little while ago," Faith told her. "Anyway, it's turned into spring outside."

Indeed, the temperature had climbed almost to sixty, and the sun beat down with springlike warmth out of a cloudless sky. Water trickled steadily from the eves of the cabin. And the river was swollen beyond its banks, it's color light as air.

Leaning a little on Lucy's arm, Faith trudged down to the dock, with its new boards in place. Here she stood, taking deep searching breaths of the pine scented air.

"I just love the air here," she told Lucy. "It's so clean and pure. Does thee suppose it will someday get polluted too?"

"Probably so," Lucy said gloomily. "From everything I read we are just about doomed."

"Doomed by our greed," Faith said. "Somehow, after everything that has gone before, I can't believe it's all going to end up so, so ignominiously."

"What does thee mean about everything that has gone before?" Lucy asked.

"O, I don't know," Faith said, "the valor of our ancestors for one thing. And whatever it is that urges people to spend themselves for some larger purpose. The sense we've had that it all matters, somehow."

"I've never been able to believe it does," Lucy confessed.

"You did that summer you went to workcamp," Faith reminded her. "But lately thee's been too worried." A quick hurt look crossed Lucy's face. "Thee's had too many things to worry about," Faith amended. "Does thee mind if we sit down on the bench. My back won't take this any more."

Lucy helped Faith to sit down, then joined her, sighed, and fixing her eyes on the river began to kick fretfully at the melting snow on the dock. A large chunk fell off the edge, and melted quickly in the water. Nearby a chickadee began his winter song.

"I don't know that I'm going to be able to continue to hold my marriage together," she at last blurted out. "It hasn't been good for years, as perhaps thee has realized. But now Bert's got a young lady friend, actually a former secretary, with whom he's very much involved. He's just hanging on for the sake of the children. And since Jennifer is getting to be such a women's lib person, he thinks hanging on is a mistake."

Faith took her mittened hand. "How so?" she asked.

"O, confused reasoning," Lucy said. "He thinks this is all an act of rebellion on Jennifer's part. That she is getting the brunt of our poor relationship, and is retaliating. And of course as he gets more and more conservative, everything that goes wrong he blames on my Quaker liberalism."

Faith laughed. "I hardly think of thee as a Quaker liberal. In fact, we Smedleys have been rather conservative ourselves, I'd say."

"He thinks thee is turning into some sort of radical in thy old age," Lucy admitted miserably.

"Perhaps I am," Faith said. "I've always been a late bloomer." She looked at Lucy's anguished face, and decided it was no time for levity. "Does thee truly want to hold the marriage together?" she asked sympathetically.

"I don't know," Lucy said slowly. "Until recently I never conceived of doing anything else. I thought it was my duty. We do have four children. Besides, where would I go and what would I do with myself if I weren't Bert's wife? It's all I know."

"But if it is really miserable for both of you it can't be good for your children," Faith said. "And thee's really young enough to start a whole new career. Forty-seven is just the beginning, these days."

Lucy laughed shortly. "Is my Quaker mother counseling divorce?"

"I can't know how thee feels about Bert so I can't counsel thee," Faith said. "I do know I have the feeling that thee has never had a chance to be thyself. And its partly my fault, I'm sure. Problems in my marriage rubbed off on thee."

"What problems?" Lucy said. "I always thought of thee and Dad as very happy."

"We were, from time to time," Faith said. "But we had our troubles. Thy father had been raised to be very reserved. It was hard for him to be close to anyone, even his wife. And when I was young I found I needed more. So I was the errant one in our family. I fell in love with someone else."

Lucy stared at her. "It's hard for me to imagine that," she said. "Well, falling in love, yes. But doing something about it?"

"It's hard for me to tell thee about it," Faith admitted. She felt her cheeks grow warm with blood, and her heart seemed to be beating much too quickly. For so many years she had kept this secret to herself. "But thee was so close to thy father I always felt that somehow, some of the hurt got dumped on thee when thee was a little girl. I felt guilty."

"When did this happen?" Lucy asked.

"It began just a year after we were married," Faith told her. "That's when I met this other person. And I never entirely got over thinking about him."

"It was sort of a fantasy?" Lucy ventured.

"No, it was real enough. The year we lived in England I saw him again, and things came to a head. I told thy father about it, and he offered to let me go, but of course he was sad, and then, I had you children to think about." She paused, staring at the river. "I'm making it sound too simple. This person, this other man was married too. He felt sure his wife couldn't cope with his leaving her."

"Thee's never told anyone a word about this?" Lucy asked.

"No, I felt too bad about it," Faith told her. "Thy father was so hurt, and I worked hard at making it up to him. But I saw that something had happened to thee. It was on the boat back from England that I first noticed that thee had a worried look."

"That was the year I started having nightmares, wasn't it?" Lucy asked.

"Yes," Faith said. "Isn't that funny? I had completely forgotten."

They looked at each other, squinting against the dazzling light to read each other's faces. Nearby a nuthatch squawked.

"All the therapy I had, and I never knew," Lucy said slowly.

"I guess I should have told thee long ago," Faith said. "I was afraid it would hurt thy father further if anyone else knew. And then, of course, he had to pay me back. He had to try having an affair. We had a very hard time for a while."

"I had no idea," Lucy said.

"It happens a lot. A lot more than people think. Yes, even in some Quaker marriages," Faith said. "It's not the end of the world, though it feels like it at the time." She got up slowly to ease her back. "Let's walk for a bit, shall we? I want to look at the land around the bridge."

Lucy took her arm, and they walked slowly along the river bank, trudging through the soft snow to follow the familiar path through the bush laurel. Though the river was too deep and swift for swimming, it widened out into a shallow pool under the bridge at the beginning of the blueberry fields. Here the Smedley children one by one had learned to wade, then to put their heads under water, and finally to dogpaddle frantically into the current. While the land belonged to the Whites, they had invited the neighbors up and down the creek to share it, so that several generations of Swallow Creek summer residents had also learned to swim here. After swimming it was nice to sit in the sun on the sloping sandy banks, and to share a picnic lunch. Swallow Creek residents had enjoyed many a Fourth of July picnic at this spot.

Today, the creek was swelling with the runoff from the January thaw, but ice crystals still hung from the bridge. Faith walked up the bank to a distance of about fifty feet, and looked around appraisingly. There was a nice large jack pine, and a sweet gum on the property.

"This would make a nice housesite," she said to Lucy.

"Is thee thinking of building?" Lucy asked

"I might," Faith said, "I just might."

"Don't you think we ought to be getting back?" Lucy asked cautiously. "I think these boots must leak. My feet are wet and cold."

"Yes, let's go back," Faith said. She was glad for Lucy's strong arm, and felt a rush of love for this oldest daughter of hers. Poor child, poor child, what did I do to thee so many years ago?

Later that night Lucy returned to the subject. Faith had gone to bed early and was sitting propped up with pillows, reading. Lucy perched at the foot of the bed.

"I've been thinking about what thee said this afternoon," she began.

"I'm sure it was a shock," Faith said. "Buried things have the potential of doing great harm."

"If thee really loved this other man, thee must have been very brave to give him up," Lucy said. "Thee must have suffered a lot."

"Yes, that's true," Faith said. "It faded finally, but there were days I remember when it was just a matter of getting through them, one hour at a time. And Tom, thy father, looking so hurt and acting so withdrawn, I couldn't go to him for comfort. Or he to me. I'm realizing I was just too preoccupied to pay much attention to thee or the other children for that matter."

Lucy waved her hand impatiently. "But after all that buried pain, look what thee has done with thy life," she exclaimed. "Does thee realize how many people look up to thee as someone special?"

Faith looked at her keenly. "Don't turn me into an argument for silent suffering. I really didn't think I had any options. But who knows, it might have been better for everyone if I had struck out."

"Thee doesn't go in for easy answers, does thee?" Lucy asked.

"I've never found any," Faith told her. She paused. "I don't want thee to regard this as an argument for sticking out a bad marriage. But Tom and I eventually found each other again, and we had many many happy years."

Lucy sighed, got up from the bed, and walked to the window. The night outside was clear and radiant with stars. It had grown colder, and the snow sparkled in the light.

"I've been thinking about going back to school and getting a degree in history," she said. "I've always loved it so."

"That sounds like a fine idea." Faith said.

"I don't know how Bert will react," Lucy said.

"Thee'll just have to see," Faith said. "Maybe if thee's more thy own woman it will make things better between you two. Or if the marriage needs to end, it will bring the end closer. Thee will just have to proceed as way opens."

"I've always liked that saying but I never felt I could apply it to myself," Lucy said. "I've always wanted to see the way ahead."

"I've been reading about an ancestor of ours who refused to plan anything," Faith told her. "She left it all up to Divine guidance. Even what skirt to wear. I'm not like that. But I do proceed a lot on feelings."

Lucy turned away from the window, and began brushing her hair. In the light from the bedlamp she looked younger, less lined. "It would be so nice to stop being worried all the time," she admitted. "To leave things up to chance or fate, or the Light, or whatever. I wonder if I can ever learn to do that?"

"Get started with thy history studies," Faith said. "That sounds to me like a right leading. Remind me in the morning, and I'll give thee the journal of Lydia White to take home and read."

After they had said goodnight and Lucy had gone off to her bed, Faith lay for sometime with her eyes open, looking out at the glittering winter stars. Was it possible that all her years of worrying over Lucy had been the price she had paid for Alex? For loving him in the first place? Or for giving him up? It was very difficult to know. I shouldn't be struggling to understand myself at this age, she thought. I should be composing my mind for death. But I'm getting nowhere fast in that direction. I'll never live to see if Lucy completes her degree, or patches up her marriage or becomes her own woman at last.

Don't thee go feeling sorry for thyself, Faith warned. But the distant stars began to dance before her eyes in a maze of tears.

Chapter 13

FEBRUARY 21, 1969

t snowed heavily again in early February, and the snow plow came clanking down the lane to Faith's cabin once more. But in a couple of weeks this snow too began to melt, and soon the ground was bare except for some dirty patches of old snow in deep shadow. Everywhere there was a constant dripping and burbling of water, foretelling the approach of spring. Faith noticed that the buds on the blueberry bushes were growing rosier, and that the maples had begun to show a faint redness against the sky. It was a full year since her operation, and here she still was, weaker, more painridden, but still alive to her senses, able to enjoy at least part of each beautiful day.

As soon as the soil dried out, Juan Costa was going to dig the footings for a cabin on the bend of the river. She had talked to the township office, and a man had come out to test the soil for percolation, so that she could put in plumbing. The verdict was positive. The sceptic tank would have to be set 100 feet back from the river, which would be expensive, but not impossibly so. She had also talked to a man at Brown's Mills who dug wells. He had assured her that there was a good vein of water on her land, and he should have no difficulty. Otherwise, water could be pumped from her own well, but that would be expensive and cumbersome.

"Thee realizes, doesn't thee, that thee will set the Swallow Creek Association on its ear?" David asked Faith.

"Just because I am building a small cabin on my own land?" Faith asked innocently. "It will be out of sight of any other cabin on the river, won't it? Up here at the end of the preserve? We're obeying all the regulations, aren't we?"

"But who is going to live in it?" David asked. "Remember, the association has a right to pass on the tenants, too."

"Is that in our deed?" Faith asked.

"No, but it's a long standing gentleman's agreement."

Faith smiled, thinking of Abigail. "Fortunately, I am not a gentleman," she said.

David hesitated. "And how much is it going to cost?" he asked. "Thy principal isn't endless, as I'm sure thee is aware."

"Well, I won't be needing it much longer," Faith pointed out. "And anyway, I expect some donations."

"From whom?"

"From John Randall, for one. There may be others."

"Randall? Thee must be crazy."

"Not really," Faith smiled. "Come into the garage with me. I have something to show thee."

After rebuilding her woodshed, Juan Costa had constructed a workbench along one side of the garage to hold his tools. At one end was a cardboard box containing some blackened pots and pans, remnants of the fire.

153

Faith fished around in the box, then drew out a length of frayed electric cable.

"I went over to the cabin site with Angelina last week to see if we could find anything in the ashes worth rescuing, and I found this beneath the pole."

"Mother, thee surprises me," David said. "Surely thee knows that wouldn't hold up as evidence in a court of law."

"But think about the publicity. Think what the people at the Moorestown country club would say," Faith said innocently.

"So what does thee intend to do?"

"I already did. Harriet drove me to Moorestown and I showed this to John Randall."

"And?"

"And, he blustered for a time, and then he agreed to make a contribution to a new cabin."

"And did thee tell him where thee intended to build the cabin?"

"One thing at a time," Faith said innocently.

"I thought the Costas had a place to live in Camden," David said, switching his tactics.

"Yes, but they like it better here," Faith told him. "And he's working in Mt. Ephraim now on the days he's not at the center. Sylvia Shipley got him a job repairing the meeting house, and then one of the members needed a new porch. He's a good workman."

"Mother, thee is incorrigible," David said. "Thee is supposed to be resting and reflecting instead of starting a new crusade."

"I have been reflecting," Faith said. "And as a result, way opened."

David left, chuckling. But a few days later he called, sounding concerned.

"I hate to tell thee this, but thy new cabin has turned into a big issue," he said. "Someone from down there, I think it must be Paxton, has called the members, and they've been calling me. John Newell has just left my office."

"The Newells haven't been down here once in the past four years," Faith said. "What possible harm do they think I might be going to do them?"

"Property values," David said. "Everyone is worried about property values. That and the fact that the Swallow Creek community is so fragile and so precious they hate to see it menaced."

"By putting a nice, decent Puerto Rican couple near the river?" Faith said. "Really!" she turned away from the phone, sick at heart.

Later that afternoon she had a call from Jennifer, in her Cambridge apartment.

"Grandmere! I worry about thee so, and then thy voice sounds so nice and normal over the phone."

"I am nice and normal," Faith said. "Most of the time, that is. How is thee?"

"I'm fine," Jennifer said. "Next weekend I'm going to Washington with my women's group to protest the Vietnam war. Thee may read about us in the papers. We're going to commit civil disobedience."

"That's exciting," Faith said. "But why just women? I thought the war affected everybody."

"But women are the ones who lose their sons and lovers," Jennifer said heatedly, "and they are the ones who are brainwashed into making wars possible."

"That's true," Faith admitted. "Thee sounds like one of thy ancestors. Her name was Abigail. I'd like thee to read her journal some day."

"Was she a suffragist?" Jennifer asked.

"Presuffragist," Faith said. "But Jennifer, be sure to wear warm clothing. Winter underwear. I am told the jails are sometimes pretty cold."

"Lorene said that," Jennifer said. "She was in jail a lot in Birmingham during the early civil rights days."

"And who is Lorene?" Faith asked.

"My new roommate," Jennifer said. "She's neat. She's a Black feminist. There aren't a whole lot of those."

"I'd love to meet her," Faith said.

"I want thee to, " Jennifer said. "Could I bring her to Swallow Creek during spring break?" "Of course," Faith said.

They said goodbye, and Faith went to her seat by the window and sat staring at the water a long time. Then she went to the phone to call her lawyer.

The next day Sylvia Shipley called. "Will thee be home next First Day afternoon?" she asked. "John and Sarah Newell and I would like to drop in. The Newells want to see thee, old dear, but they also want to talk over some Swallow Creek business."

"I'll be here," Faith said, sick at heart. She hadn't expected Sylvia, of all people, to oppose her.

"I'm not sure that I am going to be able to bear it," she confided to Harriet after she had hung up. "They are all lifelong friends. I don't want to hear them say the things I know they are going to say."

"Don't let them come," Harriet urged. "Call Sylvia back and say no. They have no business upsetting thee when thee isn't feeling well. I don't understand people at all. All that sympathy when thee was first ill. And now when thee's worse they seem to have forgotten all about anything but their selfish interests."

"No, I have to see this through," Faith said. "Life isn't about running away from problems, whatever else it's about. But Harriet, I want thee to scat. Call Rachel and have dinner with thy grandchildren. I don't want thee here at all. David will come and give me moral support."

But even David was reluctant. "I'll come and I'll back thee up, mother," he said. "But I honestly don't agree with thee. We can't save the world from the shores of Swallow Creek. And meanwhile I don't see why thee has to get into these complicated matters when thee ought to be . . . to be resting."

Faith thought about Lydia White Morris's exercises over the fear of death. She had believed the Lord needed her for further service. Maybe the Lord needed Faith too. But He couldn't require her services very much longer. In the last week, the old familiar pain had gotten a good deal worse. She hadn't yet mentioned it to anyone, but she had made an appointment to see Frank Stoddard early in the week, and she was taking the maximum number of pain killers he had given her.

Sunday dawned clear and almost springlike. By mid-morning it was so warm in the sun that Faith took a camp chair down to the dock. The twitter of chickadees and nuthatches and the sheen of the sun on the water lulled her, and filled her with an inexpressible joy. She watched a twig leap to and fro in the tug of the current, and saw how the water parted to form a silver triangle around it. How easy, she thought, to slip out of a tired old aching self, and become a drop of that leaping stream. And I will, she reminded herself, I soon will. Yes, it was possible to become excited about dying.

David came after lunch, a little earlier than the rest. Faith thought he looked heavier, not in body but in spirit, more middle-aged than she had ever seen him. He was a good, conscientious man, she thought, struggling to find rational solutions in a world that had little reason in it.

"Thee's not to worry about my affairs," she told him. "What I am doing may not seem very sensible to thee, but I feel as though I have a leading, as the old Quakers used to say."

"I don't remember thy ever saying that before," David said.

"I don't know that I've ever felt it before," Faith confided. "And David, I just decided this morning. I don't want to be buried with all those Smedleys at Brook Run Meeting. I want my ashes scattered right down here. I'm sure Tom would understand."

Promptly at three Sylvia and the Newells arrived. Faith gave them tea and waited patiently while they exchanged gossip about mutual friends; who was ill, who had died, who had moved to Florida.

Finally, John Newell broached the subject. "We understand thee is thinking of building a cabin at the bend," he remarked pleasantly.

"I'm going to build it this very spring," Faith said. "We'll start as soon as the ground is ready. David has the plans here to show you. It will be set back further than most cabins on the river. I think it conforms to all the rules of the association."

John Newell made a deprecating gesture. "Faith, anything thee does is always in good taste, and always sensitive to others," he said. "We who know thee know that. It's just that there are some new members who don't know thee quite so well, and there's been some talk, some concern. We thought it right to come directly to thee in true Quaker fashion rather than having it hang over us all."

"Is it because I was thinking of having the Costas occupy it?" Faith said helpfully. She knew she seemed calm, but her heart was beginning to pound.

"No one seems to know exactly what thy plans for occupancy were," John Newell said uncomfortably.

"Well, I am not absolutely sure myself," Faith said. "I am offering to rent it to the Costas, but they seem a bit reluctant. They say they don't want to make waves."

"See, I told thee," Sylvia said excitedly to John Newell. "Faith would never force anyone into an awkward situation just to prove a point."

"John knows that," Sarah Newell answered Sylvia irritably. "He's just got to be in a position to reassure the association members at that special meeting."

"Special meeting?" Faith asked.

"It's not that any of the members are the least bit prejudiced," Sylvia rushed on, addressing herself to Faith and ignoring Sarah. "I'm sure thee knows that. The Barclays have brought down a Negro student from Germantown Friends and we've had Spring Street community picnics here. Well, I certainly needn't tell thee that. Thee's helped to sponsor them. But there are some members who are just a tiny bit concerned that if we start to rent or to sell to local people we might soon be overwhelmed."

"It just seems best to stick to the rules and keep the properties in the hands of people we know," John explained.

"What about the Stromans?" Faith asked. "No one knew them, did they? And what about the people who bought the Stevenson place. Aren't they from Mullica Hill? Isn't that local?"

"But they are all nice, quiet people," Sarah said. "Our sort of people. The concern is about getting a different element in here. I'm sure your couple is nice and quiet, but there's the old question of what happens when they bring their friends."

Sylvia shot Sarah an angry glance. "Faith and I have heard that argument at the community center a thousand times and we don't like it one bit," she said testily.

"Then what does thee think?" Faith asked Syliva curiously.

"It's just one of those modern dilemmas," Sylvia said. "Of course in theory we ought to welcome the Costas. But it really might be the end of Swallow Creek as we know it. Thee wasn't here six years ago when we had all that trouble with local teenagers breaking into the cabins and vandalizing them. We had to call the police repeatedly, although it was against our principles to do so. But if we want to keep the place the way it is, with the birds and the peace we all love so, without beer cans and transistor radios all over the place, we have to face some unpleasant truths."

"I had thought having the Costas here would protect us," Faith said. "He could serve as a watchman, and help all the residents with repairs. And then in the summer, when the migrants are here, they could supervise the little beach so the children could swim there."

"Swimming in the creek?" John Newell said. "See, Sylvia, I told thee it would come to that."

"Maybe we've had the creek to ourselves too long," Faith said, her heart pounding. "Maybe it's time for it to belong to the people who may not appreciate it exactly as we do, but may need it more."

"But mother, then thee wouldn't have had this peaceful year thee has loved so," David reminded her.

"I've thought about that," Faith said. "If it has been wrong, I've been part of the wrong. Am part of the wrong. Quakers have always tried to do the right thing. But this land we love was taken from the Indians, and we live comfortably along today at the expense of the rest of the world, just like everyone else. I'm seventy-six, and I'm just beginning to wake up and see that."

Sylvia's eyes filled with tears and her lips trembled. "I think this is an awful thing we have done to come down here and bother Faith with our little anxieties," she said tremulously. "Especially when we don't know who is going to live in the cabin. I think we ought to apologize. I do. Apologize and go home." She reached into her purse for a handkerchief and dried her eyes.

"Sylvia is right," John said heavily. "People got over-wrought. We did hear that the Costas had a nephew who might cause trouble."

"No, it was right to come," Faith said gently. "And to raise the issues. We all need to wrestle with them, God knows. Whether or not the Costas decide to rent the cabin, I'm leaving it to my grandchildren. But it's with the understanding that they will share it with their friends of whatever color. And I want them to allow the migrant children to use the beach in the summer. I'll not have them chained to any old gentleman's agreement. I've put that in my will."

There was absolute silence in the cabin. Sylvia blew her nose and dried her eyes briskly. Even David looked shocked.

"I've been reading my family papers this winter," Faith went on. "Some of them are very dull, but once in a while I came across a man or a woman who was really turned on by the Holy Spirit, and inevitably such a person didn't care much about his or her possessions. They didn't need things, because they had a greater treasure. That's what we've lost. That's what I hope our grandchildren will find again one way or another. I want them free to search."

"But Faith," Sarah began.

"It's settled," Faith said pleasantly. "I've signed the codicil. And now, if you will excuse me, I'm afraid I must lie down."

David saw them to the door, and came back to say goodbye.

"I wish thee had said something to me about thy will," he said. "They are all going to be in a tizzy now. Think of the phone calls, the committee meetings, the petitions."

"And eventually they'll all come down piously on the wrong side," Faith said. "At least I am afraid they will."

"Probably," David agrees, "if thee means the side that opposes thee."

"Well let them," Faith said. "For once I've done the right thing. I just hope all the bother won't fall on thee."

David made an impatient gesture. "It's not that, and thee knows I don't care a hoot about the property," he said. "But I do care a hoot about thee having a little peace right now."

"I've got it," Faith said. "The peace that passeth understanding. Or some simple Quaker alternative. But run along now, dearie. I'm very tired."

Chapter 14

MARCH 28, 1969

All through the first weeks of March it rained intermittently. The sky was colorless behind the thickening buds of the maples, the mosses along the waterside were brilliantly green, the blueberry bushes, vivid with rising sap. Mergansers on their northern migration landed on the river and rose in a whirr of wings. There was a sweet, swampy smell from the marshes, and the red-winged blackbirds called their haunting "whee-whee" from the tall grasses.

The river, still clear and colorless as the sky above it, rose and rose. Every day another familiar landmark disappeared in the watery expanse. The twists and turns of the river bed were smoothed away—it was all a single sheet of deceptively quiet looking water. People began to talk about the famous floods Swallow Creek had seen. Remember the time the bridge was washed away? Remember when the Nicholson place was flooded out?

Faith watched her own dock disappear, and the water creep daily nearer the cabin steps. They were on high ground; never had the White cottage been flooded. Still, the remorselessly advancing water was eery and depressing. It reminded her of the advancing disease now active in her own body.

She had been to see Frank the day after the visit from the Newells and Sylvia Shipley. He ran some tests, and a few days later, when she returned to hear the results, and insisted that she needed to know the exact truth, he confirmed her suspicions that the cancer was active again and had spread up and down her intestinal tract.

"I'll step up the chemotherapy if you like," he told her. "It will make you feel worse for a while, and it may have unpleasant side effects, but it will slow down the process."

"What side effects?" Faith wanted to know.

"You'll be nauseous, and some of your hair might fall out," Frank explained.

"It's been doing that already," Faith admitted. "I must say I don't enjoy the thought of ending my days wearing a wig. Is it up to me? The higher dosage, I mean, not the wig?"

Frank hesitated. "Naturally, I am conditioned to want to do anything in my power to halt the disease. But that's what it would be, a delaying action."

"Just slow it down a bit?"

Frank nodded. "Buying time. Of course there are new discoveries all the time, as well as spontaneous remissions no one can explain," he added.

Faith considered. She was growing tired of the battle. And yet there was still so much to get settled, so much to think about.

"I'll take at least one course of the stronger medicine," she decided, "see how it goes."

At Frank's suggestion she stayed with David and Margaret for the first three days, fighting continuous nausea and dizziness in their guest bedroom. Then, armed with a new and stronger painkiller and pills to settle her stomach, she returned to Swallow Creek.

In the long gray rainy days she grew accustomed gradually to a new pace of living revolving around her illness. She who had always bounced up in the morning now lay in bed, listening to Harriet's bustle in the kitchen, wondering whether or not she could face the smells of Harriet's breakfast. All her life she had enjoyed good food. Now meals were something to get though as quickly and painlessly as possible. She ate junkets and custards and gruels, a few spoonsful at a time, hoping to catch her wary and rebellious stomach off guard.

When she finally got up, it became a matter of husbanding her strength, making the trip from bed to her seat by the window with care, learning to ask Harriet to bring her her glasses or her fountain pen if she had left them behind, rather than hopping up to fetch them. She tried to use what little energy she had in the mornings to work on her correspondence. A stream of letters from England, from France, from Germany, from former Algerian comrades, as well as from classmates and friends scattered all over the United States had continued to arrive all winter at Swallow Creek. Many she had put off writing for weeks, knowing it would be the last time she would be able to reach out to her friends, and wanting to make these letters special. Now, however, she was aware that time was very short. She wrote quick, warm notes, as many as six or eight a morning, saying little about her present circumstances, stressing happy shared memories. She wrote to Priscilla and Marguerite and Isabel, remembering happy times last summer. Let her friends at least know, when they heard of her death, that she had thought of them.

By noon she was exhausted enough to return to her bed, and sometimes there would be the blessed respite of a short nap, helped along she supposed by the pills Frank had given her to take at lunchtime. Then back to the chair by the window for the afternoon, to read the White papers and watch the river flow by.

She was now reading the journal of her grandfather, Samuel White, who had kept store and taught school in southern New Jersey. His life seemed to be one of constant loss; first his young wife, then his daughter, then his father and mother, then a brother. Throughout his journal he struggled for resignation to the Divine will which had inflicted these sorrows upon him. "I believe we cannot possess true peace or a solid comfort here, except we are obedient to the admonitions and stirrings of the spirit of Christ within us," he wrote. These stirrings, however, did not seem to have sent her grandfather into action, as they had some of her ancestors. He regretted the Civil War, in which he could play no part as a conscientious and peace loving Friend. He seemed, however, untouched by the abolitionist sentiment that had so stirred his cousin, Abigail. "Returned home from our yearly meeting, the awful news of war being so much around the city during our meeting; it brought sorrow, I believe, to the hearts of many. By this judgment of the Lord over our country may the people be brought to learn righteousness," he wrote. Faith found his journal a trifle dull. She wondered if he were a model of the majority of Quakers of his day; pious, industrious, resigned, rather than the few activists to whom her spirit seemed to be drawn.

Still, she remembered him as a kindly presence when she was a child, taking her downtown in his horse and wagon; giving her sweets when she visited his store.

Her grandfather's reference to the yearly meeting was a reminder that she must soon decide whether or not to summon the energy to attend this year. Since the Philadelphia Yearly Meeting was first held in 1681, Whites had been attending. Faith's own father hand gone faithfully; she and Tom had attended whenever they were in the country. It was not only a time of renewal; it often served as a reunion, an opportunity to see old friends and distant cousins. Faith had posted the notice of the sessions on her desk, and looked at it every day, wondering if she could manage at least one afternoon session.

Harriet of course begged her not to. Harriet was beginning to show the strain of constant concern. Although Angelina came to clean and cook each day, and there was little housework to do, Harriet fussed about the cabin for hours at a time, straightening the books on the shelves, or the magazines on the table, clearly unable to settle down to painting or reading. Faith knew it was Harriet's own fear of illness and of death which made her so anxious.

Still, she was not restful for Faith to be with. In another few weeks, Faith thought, she would have to find some way to tell Harriet that their time together would have to end. She must hire a practical nurse, and would need Harriet's bedroom. It was either that, or move in with Margaret and David. They had been urging her both to hire a nurse and to come to them. Margaret had two rooms and a bath on the second floor which she was holding ready for such a decision.

In the fourth week of March she began to feel a little better. She awoke one morning to a flood of spring sunshine in her bedroom, and a feeling of inner lightness she had not had for some time. "Have died and gone to heaven," she told herself, remembering Tom. What a good joke on the human race if there really were a heaven after all! What a predicament if she were to arrive and find both Tom and Alex waiting for her!"

"I feel like going into town for the yearly meeting this evening if thee will drive me," she told Harriet when she got up. "The AFSC is reporting and there's some new work in the coal fields I want to hear about."

"Is thee really sure?" Harriet asked dubiously.

"Really sure," Faith told her.

Though the rain had at last stopped, the creek continued to rise. On the way out they had to cross a place where the road was flooded to the car's hubcaps, and turning at the bridge they saw the floodtide raging under them in a muddy torrent.

"I wouldn't like to get caught in that," Faith said, shuddering.

"A man was once drowned here," Harriet said. "Mrs. Paxton was telling me about it."

"Mrs. Paxton enjoys gloom," Faith commented.

The yearly meeting sessions were held, as always at the old Quaker meeting house at Fourth and Arch Street, built in 1804 on land which had once been used to bury the victims of yellow fever. Recently restored to fresh brightness, the old meeting house retained its serene white walls and ancient glowing pine paneling. Faith never came here without a sense of awe, left over from the time she was a little girl and clutched her father's hand as they entered this Quaker sanctuary.

They had arrived in time to sit in on the last half of the afternoon session. Faith noted that the big meeting room seemed filled with old people; white hair dominated. It took her a moment to realize that these were, of course, her contemporaries. Scattered throughout were a good many young men and women in bluejeans and long hair. It was the middle generation that was missing.

Faith and Harriet had slipped into a back bench, and hoped their arrival was not noticed. Somehow, though, the news that she had come was quickly spread. Heads turned, people waved and blew kisses. When the clerk announced the close of the afternoon session, she was besieged by old friends wanting to give her a kiss and a hug, or to squeeze her hand. Many had tears in their eyes. She was unprepared for this reception, and it was almost too much.

"I think I won't try going into the dining room," she told Margaret, who had come expressly to be with her. "I can't eat any of that food anyway. I'll lie down in the women's rest room, and perhaps thee can find me some yogurt."

The evening session was devoted to a report of the work of the American Friends Service Committee. A middle-aged man, a contemporary of David's, outlined the programs abroad: a self-help housing program in Zambia, an agricultural program in Mexico, a medical program in Chile, and a new prosthesis center in Vietnam. Tomorrow they would discuss the controversial issue of sending medical supplies to North Vietnam. Now it was time for a panel of young people to report on a new program in Appalachia.

Faith's fatigue and nausea vanished as she listened to a young woman, who did not look old enough to be out of high school, describe her work as a lawyer representing the people of the West Virginia hollows against some employment practices of the local coal company; then an even younger looking woman talk about arranging a protest at the annual meeting of the holding company which operated the strip mines. She heard in their young voices the same passion for the people and the place which she and Tom had shared during the Great Depression, when they had been sent into the area to organize feeding for the children of the unemployed miners.

"You wouldn't believe how some of those people live," a young man was now relating. "One house we visited, the roof was half off and some of the windows were out. They had tacked plastic over the holes. They had nothing to heat with but a wood stove, and they had had to chop up some of their old furniture to keep it going."

But I remember, Faith thought. She saw again the bleak, hopeless faces of the miners and their wives, and the pinched suspicious children, remembered the baby they had rushed to the nearest hospital because it was dying of malnutrition, recalled how she and Tom and the rest of the team used to choke on their own food at night, after a day spent in the midst of all that hunger and misery.

They had distributed food and organized clinics, and taught the miners to plant subsistence gardens, and tried to help revive the old mountain crafts and organized self help housing. But all along Tom had said they were not getting at the real roots of the problems. Now here was a third generation, less timid perhaps than hers, ready to do battle against the goliaths that controlled the lives of the workers, and the companies that slashed into those lovely hillsides. How happy Tom would be to hear this, Faith thought, warmed by a sense of his nearness. They had always had this between them; his deep commitment to try to make things better for people, and her pride in him for it. Alex, for all his charm, had never struck this deeper chord. Then why, at this time of her life, was she sometimes still haunted by the memory of Alex?

When the panel had finished its report she signaled to the person assigned to the roving microphone that she would like to speak. "I just wanted to say how happy I am to hear that work in the coal fields is continuing," she said in a firm voice. "Those of us who worked there, many, many years ago felt we had just scratched the surface, and that the AFSC had made a commitment to those people we must honor. Thanks for honoring it so vigorously today."

The excitement and the effort cost her heavily. She had to lean on Margaret's arm to get out to the car, while David ran interference, gently turning aside some of the old friends who wanted once more to speak to her. In the hall, she caught a glimpse of Sarah Newell; Faith thought she looked uncomfortable and wondered how the campaign to make her change her will in regard to Swallow Creek was proceeding.

"I really think thee ought to spend the night with us, mother, and go back to Swallow Creek in the morning if thee must," David said at the car. "We have a bed for Harriet too, of course. I must say thee looks terribly tired."

"No, I'll be all right," Faith assured him. "We thank thee, but I feel I need to get back there tonight, somehow."

While Harriet drove she rested her head on the back of the seat, eyes closed. There was room for neither thought nor emotion; she felt engulfed with exhaustion. How restful it was going to be to die.

At the bridge over Swallow Creek, Harriet slowed with an exclamation, and Faith's eyes jerked open. There were floodlights down at the edge of the water, and men running to and fro.

"Pull over, Harriet," Faith said, her heart beating wildly. She rolled down her window and asked a policeman standing on the bridge what the matter was.

"Some little kid fell in upstream," the man said. "We're trying to recover the body before it goes over the falls."

Faith started to ask the man if he knew the name of the child. But it was not necessary. Down below the bridge, at the water's edge, she saw Susie Platt peering into the swirling torment of the river.

"We can't do anything to help, and thee is in no condition to get out of this car," Harriet cried. But Faith already had opened the door, gotten heavily to her feet, and had begun to work her way, foothold by foothold, down the slippery bank.

"I was just taking the groceries out of the car. I just turned my back for a minute," Susie told her, her eyes wide with shock. "It was just a second, really. And she's been taught never, never to go near the water. I don't think she fell in at all. I think we'll find her in the woods. We ought to be looking there."

Faith glanced at Donald, who managed to shake his head. But the confident young giant now looked as frightened and lost as a little boy.

"If anyone had to fall into the creek, it should have been me," Faith thought. She put her arms around Susie's shaking shoulders, thinking, what do I have to offer, after all my years, but the small solace of animal comfort?

A woman came down the bank toward them, carrying a folded lawn chair. Her head was tied up in a red bandana handkerchief, and she wore a man's worn leather jacket over her bathrobe. Faith recognized her as a neighbor of the Paxtons. She looked across the road to the store, and saw the couple peering anxiously from the porch.

"I saw you stop, and I thought, if that's Mrs. Smedley she ought to have a chair," the woman said. She peered at Susie Platt and her face crumbled. "You ought to come inside with me, dear. You can't do nothing here. And with the new one on its way, and all."

Susie shook her head numbly. Donald stared at the men, who had gathered in a particular spot, and were shining their lights on something that bobbed in the water. Then he snatched Susie and turned her roughly so that her face was pressed against his jacket. Faith sat down heavily on the proffered chair, and the lights began to swim in huge arcs before her eyes. She seemed to be falling immense distances while the woman's voice echoed in her ear, "Now if you'll just put your head between your legs, dear. . . . Just give me a hand with her, will you, Mrs. Buffum?"

No, Faith told herself, I won't faint. She took a long, shuddering breath of the night air, gagged with nausea, then straightened, and got to her feet. Harriet stood on one side of her, the neighbor woman on the other. Donald was leading Susie away. Across the water, the men had retrieved a small bright bundle from the water.

I am persuaded that my dear daughter now knows a sweeter peace than she had ever known on earth, Samuel White had written. He had written that in anguish, Faith suddenly knew. The anguish now was having nothing to offer Susie and Donald. But she would do her poor best. She could at least sit with them that night.

"I feel much better now," she told her attendants. "I'll be all right as soon as I get to the car. Harriet, can thee help me? And thank you for being so kind."

Chapter 15

April 22, 1969

perating on will power alone, Faith managed to spend some time each day for the next week with Susie Platt. There was not much she could find to say to the grieving girl, but Susie seemed to find some comfort in her mere presence. When relatives and friends came to express condolences, Faith withdrew and lay on the Platts crumbled bed, looking out at the river.

The memorial service was to be held at the little Rancocas meeting house, opened especially for this occasion. With a last burst of energy, Faith managed to attend the heartbreaking meeting, but found she could not rise to speak, as she had hoped she would be led to do. She lay back in the car exhausted on the way home. As soon as she was able to rally a little strength she called David to come and get her.

"Harriet, dear, I think it's time for thee to make other plans," she told her old friend softly as they waited for David to arrive. "I don't know if I'll be coming back here at all. And if I do, I think I'll have to have a practical nurse. Margaret has found a good sensible woman."

Harriet began to cry, the muted tears of the old. "I want to stay," she objected. "I want to help thee and I know how better than any old nurse. And Faith, this is very selfish, but I want to be with thee. There's no one in the whole world who cares a thing about me any more but thee, Faith. The children try to be patient with me, but to them I'm just an old nuisance most of the time. We only connect when we talk about things in the past. Thee's the only one who still makes me feel like a real living human being. I'll learn how to do things for thee if thee needs nursing. I don't mind."

"Yes, thee does mind," Faith told her gently. "I've seen thee flinch when I've thrown up, and it's going to get a lot worse. I need someone around me who's used to ill and dying people and doesn't care much, one way or the other."

Harriet finally agreed tearfully, and at Faith's suggestion called her sister in Cincinnati to arrange a visit. David arrived and took Faith straight to University Hospital, where she spent five nightmarish, confused days in treatment. Then, feeling wobbly but better, she returned to Swallow Creek with Elsa Parks, a large honey-colored woman with a soft manner and strong arms.

In the pile of mail awaiting her at the cabin was a letter from Beth. "Mother says thee isn't very well so perhaps this isn't going to work," Beth wrote. "But remember when thee asked me to come down in April? Well, I want to come. Only not with Rich. We've broken up and I'm having a hard time getting over it. Mother is good about not saying anything, but I can feel her hurting almost as much as I do. I can count on thee, grandmere, to listen but not to be so sad."

"Come," Faith wired back. "Come as soon as possible."

Spring had at last arrived at Swallow Creek, though the budded branches were still bare. Trailing arbutus blossomed in the woods, the small pixie mosses were in bloom, and black and white and myrtle warblers twittered in the pines. The days were mild and sunny, and Faith liked to have Elsa set up her lawn chair on the deck, and help her down into it, so she could sit and watch the river, now flowing primly between its banks, as it wound endlessly past her.

At the bend in the river, Juan was at work on the new cabin. She could hear his hammering from time to time. At noon Angelina took him his lunch, and returned to report on his progress. One day she and Juan drove to Mt. Ephraim and chosen windows. She smiled as she described the beveled glass they had settled upon for the front door.

Faith had heard nothing further from the residents association. Perhaps the drowning of the Platt child had awakened the consciences of her Swallow Creek neighbors, Faith thought. Or maybe they had decided to postpone the battle until after her death. Well, let them. It was possible that at least some of her children might be influenced by the wishes of the community, but she was pretty confident her grandchildren would not. She thought she had been rather clever to leave the cabin itself to a younger generation.

It would be nice, though, to live long enough to see the Costas living in the new cabin, and to watch the children of migrants bathe in the river. But that would mean living for at least three more months, and she knew that was unlikely, now.

Beth came down by bus, and Elsa Parks drove into town to get her. Faith was shocked to see how thin Beth was, and how woebegone she looked. Though she was still a replica of her mother, she was smaller and sadder than Anne had ever been. Faith's heart went out to her with a lurch.

"O, it smells so good here," Beth exclaimed, after kissing Faith gently. "And it's so quiet. Why do people live in such smelly, noisy places? I just know that in a place like this I could get it all together."

"There's a wonderful peace here," Faith agreed. "It comes out and greets one."

"O grandmere, I'm a selfish pig!" Beth exclaimed. "I know thee's not feeling well, and thee's gotten so thin and pale! I really shouldn't have come like this."

"I wanted thee to," Faith told her. "I know I look awful but I feel better already. Thee just mustn't mind if at times I get fussy from the pills I have to take."

"I won't mind," Beth told her. She slipped off her loafers and put one toe into the river. "That's not really too cold. Maybe later in the day I'll swim."

Faith fought back the impulse to tell her to be careful. The White grandchildren had all swum in the river since they were very little, and knew its strong currents. The Platt tragedy might have happened anywhere. Still, she felt a little anxious when Beth set out alone in the canoe that afternoon. The girl's depression and the treacherous river seemed a bad combination.

Although the pain was strong, she put off taking her 3 PM pill until Beth returned; then took it and went to bed for a long nap. She awakened in the late afternoon, feeling woozy, and called Elsa to help her get up and down to her chair on the dock. The day had grown unseasonably warm; around eighty, she guessed. Beth, wearing a bikini, was stretched out on a blanket. She had her sketch pad and a pencil in front of her, but was simply staring into the current.

"Did thee swim?" Faith asked her.

"Yes," Beth said. "It was lovely. I was able to lose myself in the water for a little while."

"We came down here our senior year at Westtown at this time," Faith reminisced. "And it was hot like this. Our chaperone had a fit, but we insisted on swimming. We had those old woolen scratchy suits. The water was cold, but it was lovely then, too."

"Was grandpere there?" Beth asked curiously.

"Yes, he was there," Faith said. "Clowning about, making sure that everyone had a chance to laugh."

"I envy thee, marrying someone thee fell in love with at high school," Beth said wistfully. "Thee must have nothing but happy memories, now."

Faith snorted. "Life is never that simple," she said. "At least it never has been for me, or for anyone I know. No, they aren't all happy memories. Tom and I got married right after he graduated from college and we were babes in the woods, and at first the sex part wasn't right and we were both bewildered and unhappy about that. That's something your generation doesn't have to contend with."

Beth rolled over and looked at her curiously. "But it got all right eventually?"

"Yes, but by then I'd gotten my feelings entangled with someone else. I didn't do anything about it, but I kept thinking about him for years. And all the time I loved your grandfather more and more, and saw how hurt he was and how he suffered in silence. I hated that, too."

"Grandmere! I had no idea such a thing could ever happen to anyone so together as thee is!" Beth stared at her in amazement. "Did thee consider divorce?"

"In those days one didn't think of divorce as an option. At least good Quakers didn't," Faith said. "Anyway, I didn't want to leave Tom, leave thy grandfather. I loved Tom, he was my partner for the sort of life I wanted to lead, and the father of my children. I wanted Tom, but a part of me wanted this other person too. My feeling for him was entirely different. More like a singing, a fever in the blood. When I was with him I seemed to be on a different level of consciousness. Colors were brighter, odors more powerful . . . it had nothing to do with ordinary love and with real life."

"But that is what being in love is like," Beth said. "Hadn't thee felt that way about grandpere at first?"

"No, not quite like that. I loved him, I enjoyed being with him, but there was never that flash of fire, that intuitive understanding between us. In many ways, thy grandfather was too reserved to be in love."

"What finally happened?"

"Well, actually, this man came into my life twice. Once when I had been married only a year, and then a second time, when I was in my late thirties and had all of my children. That time it became, very briefly, a real affair. But he was married too, and felt he couldn't leave his wife. Tom found out, and we went off by ourselves to the Jungfrau to try to straighten things out. I promised Tom I would never see Alex, see the man again. And shortly after that, we came home."

"O grandmere, that must have been hard."

"Promising was easy; but the hard part came later," Faith said. "Getting through each hour or each day was a struggle for a long time. And I got sick, which was no help. But thy grandfather was patient, and the children were loving, and somehow I managed to recover."

"How long did it take?" Bath asked wistfully. "To begin to feel normal again, I mean?"

Faith hesitated. "A long time," she said gently. "But I was much older than thee is now. The habit of loving is harder to break the older you get."

"But thee did get completely over it?"

"Not completely," Faith said frankly. "When thee has felt that deeply thee is imprinted for life, in many ways. It opens one up to life, maybe even to the Light. Thee is a different person afterward. There is no turning back."

"That's heavy," Beth said.

"When I read the journals of some of the early Quakers, they write about their religious experiences in something of the same vein," Faith said. "One woman wrote about being in love with the whole creation of God, about the herbs and the flowers speaking to her soul in a different voice. George Fox said all creation had a different smell. And they were ready to give up everything for that love; home, family, safety, everything. It must have been just as shattering."

"H'm," Beth said absentmindedly. "The thing is, I can't decide whether I really loved Rich for Rich, or for the way he made me feel. I sometimes say to myself that he was a coathanger on which I hung a lot of feelings. But whatever it was, it went deep, like thee says. And grandmere, it was he who moved out on me. He's got another woman."

Faith thought of Lucy, struggling with the same pain, as she had known it herself. "It hurts to be rejected," she said. "But maybe that's not just love but also wounded pride."

"I spend half my time planning strategies to capture him back," Beth admitted. "And then I know I wouldn't want him if he could be captured that way."

"You learn finally that you don't really need anyone," Faith said. "That needing and loving are two different things. You learn that everyone is really alone. Then you begin to be free to love and to give. But it takes a long time."

"I'm sure thee's right," Beth said. "Right now, though, I just have to get through each day somehow." She got up and stood on the edge of the dock, watching the little whirlpools and wavy patterns in the current of the golden water. Then she dove, neatly and expertly, came up downstream, sputtering, and swam with quick strokes back to the dock. "Cold," she admitted, pulling herself out in supple motion.

"Come over here and I'll dry thee," Faith said.

"O grandmere," Beth sobbed, tears suddenly mingling with the water running down her cheeks. "I feel better for a few moments, and then I feel worse again. When am I going to get over this?"

"It's hard," Faith admitted, putting her thin arm around the girl's wet body. "But thee's young and thy heart is supple like thy body. Thee'll feel better soon. I promise."

She rubbed Beth vigorously with the towel. "Now run into the cabin and get into some dry clothes," she said.

Obediently Beth left. Faith continued to sit, watching the river. Letting go of love was good practice, she thought, for letting go, as she must do, of everyone and everything. She could imagine how it had felt to dive, to feel the rippling undercurrent play like fingers along her body, to touch the murky depths, and then burst upwards toward the light.

There ought to be some pattern, some meaning to draw all this together, she thought. Her painful buried love, Beth's suffering, the drowning of the Platt child, Lucy's pain, the blooming of the sand myrtle, the song of the warblers, the flow of the water. Her Quaker ancestors had found it all so simple, it seemed. But though she admired them, no single meaning seemed to come through to her from their lives and their writings.

Unless it is just to be open to everything, she thought. Even pain, even death.

Chapter 16

MAY 25, 1969

very day she grew weaker, and her enemy, the pain, grew stronger. She took her pills every three hours now, and her life began to revolve around them; the delicious easing of pain they brought at first; the strange, confused half world into which she entered with their help; the slow fight back to consciousness as the pain took hold once more, then the long agonizing wait for the next pill.

After Beth's visit she managed for a few more days to make her slow way on Elsa Park's arm to the deck chair by the river, and there to enjoy the spring sunshine and the play of light on the water. But the weather turned cold again and there was frequent rain, and she was obliged to confine herself to her chair indoors by the window. Even that position she could tolerate for only brief periods of time. The dizziness and the ringing in her ears made it better to be flat.

One night she got up to go to the bathroom, felt dizzy, and fell beside her bed. She had to call Elsa to get up. The next day David and Margaret arrived and said they thought it was time for her and Elsa to move to their house in Chestnut Hill. She was ready to go; the pain and confusion were closing over her head now; it really did not matter after all whether the patch of sky she saw from her bed was that of Swallow Creek.

They moved her later that same day, by ambulance. The attendants were so big and burly that Faith felt ashamed of her puny, wasted flesh, but they lifted her tenderly, as though she were precious, and placed her on a stretcher. On the way from the house to the ambulance she took a deep sniff of the pine laden air. The sky was blue again this morning and a black and white warbler sang somewhere. "We'll be there when the wild blueberries are ripe," she had promised Harriet. But last summer she had been wandering in Europe and now, she would not make it. Goodbye, Faith whispered, goodbye.

At David's house they placed her in a hospital bed by the window. Here too was a patch of sky, seen through the branches of a large, budding maple. Faith enjoyed it at first, but she soon found that the brilliance hurt her eyes. She asked for the shade to be drawn, so that the window became only a patch of lighter wall in her quiet room.

Frank Stoddard came by each day now, and prescribed shots instead of pills. Faith lived both night and day in a half world of confusion. It was impossible to keep track of the days of the week; sometimes hard to decide whether it was day or night. The only reality was the monstrous pain dragging at her, trying to pull her down through a dark hole toward some deeper nightmare.

She fought against both the pain and the confusion, trying to fix her mind on other things. Sometimes she recited to herself poems she had been taught to memorize as a child, or verses from the Bible she had learned at First Day School. Sometimes she thought about Tom, or her children when they were little. Once in a while, about Alex. More and more, though, her mind kept wandering back to her own childhood. She remembered picking the long stemmed violets that grew in the orchard behind the house, or turning the crank on the ice cream freezer on the side porch, taking turns with her brother Harry, or collecting shells when the family spent the summer on the Jersey shore or cracking black walnuts before the fire on winter nights. These memories were vivid, and seemed precious and important to her. She wondered how to communicate them to the people who came and went at her bedside.

There was a constant procession of visitors, it seemed, waiting to come when she had her few lucid moments. She wondered if they were lined up at the door, each taking his or her turn. Her sister Jane came, clucking and tearful; her brother Harry, holding her hand and looking pained; Lucy and Anne, Peggy and Tim, even Charlie.

"Why Charlie, where's your beard?" she asked.

"I shaved it off to come here," he said, and she saw that his eyes were bright with tears.

Sylvia Shipley came, and was weepy, begging forgiveness. The Stromans came from Swallow Creek, bringing branches of flowering blueberry, and told her the Maryland yellow throats were singing now, and how nice the new cabin looked at the bend. Angelina Costa came, weeping, and made the sign of the cross over her bed. Jennifer arrived from Cambridge and told her that her women's group was demanding more women faculty at Harvard.

"And grandmere; mother has told me about thy will. I am so very, very proud of thee."

Faith responded to all as best she could, but theirs was a different world from hers now, a world of health and life; she was shut away in a half world of pain and approaching darkness. She felt as she had among the Algerians, before she could speak their language. There was respect and good will, but no way really to communicate with them from the country where she now lived.

Elsa Parks was nearer to her than the rest; her ally in the frequent battles with nausea as she tried to eat and drink, the humiliations of the bedpan, the anxious wait for time for another shot. Elsa seemed to know better than the others what it was like. "She's the quietest woman I ever saw to bear such pain," she heard Elsa telling Frank.

But Elsa had to sleep sometimes, and either David or Margaret now sat with her through portions of the night. Faith would awaken from her confused half sleep and see one or the other of them illuminated by the little circle of light from the reading lamp, dozing in the armchair. She hated to disturb either of them. The anxious pain in their eyes was sometimes harder to bear than the real pain inside. She had them put a clock by her bedside, and she lay at such times watching the hands move, willing the hours to pass until Elsa came back on duty with the blessed needle.

And still the pain grew stronger, more insistent. What does it want of me? Faith asked crossly. She was ready now to die. That feeling of having unfinished duties to attend had disappeared. She had lived her life, she had struggled for over a year to find its meaning, and even to communicate some of the things she had learned to her children and grandchildren. If there was more she ought to do, it was too late now. She was prepared to move on to whatever came next. But still her stubborn flesh fought against the drag of the pain toward the dark hole of oblivion.

Frank said she might have her shot whenever she wanted now; no need to wait until three hours had elapsed. Faith was grateful for the surcease, but found it meant more disorientation. The pain was still always there in the half world; a lion stalking her in the Algerian hills, a nameless dreaded thing under her trundle bed when she recalled her earliest years. It sometimes seemed better to feel the pain's full force and to fight it with the light.

The window had become the light, the oblong of illumination in her shadow world. She spent hours looking toward it with unfocused eyes, seeing the light grow and shimmer, and diminish, and sometimes throb with such intensity that it frightened her. "Mind the light," she commanded herself when the pain was at its worst. And somehow, that intense concentration on the light helped her to ride up and over the anguish.

Her childhood memories began to center on those early summers at the Jersey shore. She was a child in a black wool bathing costume, her feet and legs sprinkled with glittering particles of sand, watching her own footsteps form on the wet shingle, then be swept away by the incoming tide. Or she was in the water, swimming shoreward, struggling to reach the dry sands where her mother and brother awaited her. The pain was an octopus, pulling her downward toward the darkness, the light from the window a friendly wave lifting her, carrying her toward the shore. With each lift of the wave she felt an inexpressible delight, a tenderness toward those waiting for her; then the wave would ebb and she would be carried back, until the old enemy would grab her and pull her back toward the cold and the darkness once more.

One night she awoke to see David's head outlined by the lamplight. The pain seemed entirely gone, and she lay in delicious peace and ease, feeling such a burst of love for her son that she longed to tell him about the world in which she now had her being, the indescribable joy of the wave and its lifting. She tried to speak to him, but her voice made only a cracking sound. He startled, rose and came toward her, but as he did so the pain suddenly caught her with a force more savage than she had known before, and carried her down, down to the depths until she choked and fought for air, and then burst upward again, lung exploding, toward the light.

"Mother, what is it?" David was saying, and then she heard him running to summon Elsa, as another violent burst of pain caught her and carried her downward. But this time she discovered that instead of a dark hole what awaited her in the depths was not blackness but light, a whole ocean of light such as she had never seen before.

When the pain let go, and she shot upward once more for air, Elsa was beside her, and the rest were all standing around her. David, she saw was crying, the tears coursing down his cheeks and splashing on his collar. There was a strange rattling sound in her throat but she managed to move her lips as they bent over her. "It's all right," she whispered. "It's all the same, really."

"What does thee mean, mother?" David asked.

But it was too late to explain. She let go and allowed the pain to pull her down and down through the azure depths toward that overpowering, blinding brilliance.